Bells Will Be Ringing

Barbara Winkes

For D.

Chapter One

DANA

O ne moment, her life had been perfect. The next, it wasn't.

Perhaps there had been some signs Dana could have seen, like being late on what might be the most important day of her career. A mix of rain and snow had left a grey slush on the streets, and she wasn't going to subject her new boots to it. The first cab was snatched from her by an impolite banker type who came out of nowhere, the second by an elderly woman she couldn't say no to.

When she finally got into one, the driver managed to take the busiest route to court that got them stuck in traffic for almost half an hour.

Dana wasn't good at reading signs. She leaned back into her seat, tapped her fingers on her briefcase and daydreamed about getting out of the city for a few days.

She had put in long hours for months, hoping that she'd be named partner of the law firm Sheldon & Marks next. Her chances were excellent, the only rival left in the competition Peter Cassidy who was second chair on this case. Dana was optimistic about the outcome they expected sometime at the end of the week. After all, he had been dragging his feet the whole time and let her do most of the work. Certainly, the partners had seen it too? She wasn't too sure about Sheldon junior who was buddies with Cassidy, but his father still kept an eye on things.

Marks, as far as she knew, was in his vacation home in the Caribbean at the moment. The caseload had expanded in the past couple of years, and they needed skilled, determined lawyers. They needed *her*.

Dana cast a look at her watch, sighing in relief when the driver managed to get into a faster lane. Of all days, she needed Peter to step up. If she was lucky, the weather had delayed proceedings altogether—she couldn't be the only one who had been slowed down. Their client was a big insurance company that had been hit with a class action suit. At first, she was reluctant. However, Dana wasn't fooling herself. Sheldon & Marks wasn't exactly the firm for people who were in danger of falling through the cracks. Once she'd made a career for herself there, she could afford to go back to the ideals she'd once held. Maybe.

Their investigator had turned up information about some of the customers that had sued the insurers, suggesting the story wasn't as black and white as it seemed at first. They needed a stay to find out more, process that information. She had asked Peter to file it, and he had promised, though not without grumbling.

The cab ride was over, and Dana realized that she had left her wallet at home.

In retrospect, there had been so many signs.

·♥·♥·♥·♥·♥·

She called Tricia who was working from home on most days. No one answered. Dana was lucky to recognize a fellow attorney, Rowan Murphy, whom she'd had coffee with a few times. Asking her for money might be embarrassing, but having the driver following her around, glaring, would certainly be worse. After the verdict, she'd buy that woman all the coffee in the world.

Fortunately, Rowan proved to be understanding.

"That's okay," she said. "I know where you live."

"Thanks so much. I'll get back to you later."

"I appreciate it. Just pay me back in lattes."

"Will do. See you." Dana hastened up the stairs to the courthouse, her high heels not a good mix with the stairs made uneven by snow, ice, and salt. She averted an accident at the last moment, opened the door and all but ran to the courtroom.

Everything was going to be fine.

She knew the case inside out.

Peter had filed for a stay, and she had enough proof to argue for it. She was good at this, and by the weekend, she'd be drinking champagne with Tricia, celebrating her promotion.

Dana arrived just in time to hear the ruling—both parties had agreed to a settlement.

·♥·♥·♥·♥·♥·

An hour later, she stood in Sheldon senior's office. His son, Cassidy, and Marks were also present, the latter indication that something was horribly wrong. Only a major event would take Marks away from the golf course—something earthshaking, something threatening the foundation of the firm. The insurance provider was one of the biggest clients they had, bringing in millions for them.

Dana tried hard not to slip into panic mode. Hell, she didn't even know what panic mode looked like. All her experiences in life pointed towards the same concept. If you worked hard enough for something, you'd succeed. Always. A grade A student all through her school days, she had been hired by a prestigious law firm right out of college, worked her way up steadily. She had been dreaming of seeing her name on letterheads. Sheldon, Marks & Clover. She deserved it—or maybe she didn't, not anymore. Stop, she told herself. There was the not so small matter of Peter not filing for the stay. She had asked him to. In front of witnesses.

"As you can imagine," Sheldon senior began, "We've been fielding some angry calls. Getting angry calls from our most important client is not a good thing. They lost a lot of money with the settlement. Dana, Peter, what happened here? The case was supposed to be thrown out!"

"Well, first of all, she was late, and it wasn't the first time."

"What? That's not true!"

"It is," Cassidy claimed. "Besides, she doesn't know how to delegate, hardly ever let me do anything. I did the best I could to keep myself informed, but in the end, that wasn't enough for the judge. I'm sorry, Dana, you really messed this up."

Dana was speechless for a moment, long enough for Marks to chime in.

"I guess some damage control is in order?"

She had to find words. She had to end this nightmare. "Mr. Marks, I asked Mr. Cassidy to file for a stay. He didn't. I don't understand. The private investigator we hired had all the information—"

"The private investigator is a drunk who's about to get his license yanked," Cassidy interrupted her. "You're lucky he didn't get on the stand. Dana, what where you thinking?"

"But you told me to go with him!" It became clearer by the moment that this wasn't just a random disaster unfolding. She'd been set up.

"Ms. Clover, pointing fingers won't help at this stage. We need to come up with a solution."

"I can talk to everyone, apologize," she offered.

Sheldon junior shook his head. "This is going to take more than an apology—they will want to see gestures. Dana, Peter, go back to work, please. We'll let you know when we need you."

The moment the door fell closed behind them, Dana was confronted with the horrible possibilities. They were going to fire them both. They were going to fire her.

She wasn't sure how much influence Peter had on either decision, but she couldn't deny she had done most of the work. The responsibility rested on her shoulders, and frankly, she should have filed the damn paperwork herself. She had seen people let go over less than that...and a client that had lost millions of dollars, was waiting for an answer. A gesture. Peter had told her to hire the investigator in question. She couldn't prove it.

Perhaps there was still a way she could argue her case, or maybe there wasn't. She hadn't felt so tired in her entire life. As Peter stalked away angrily, she fell behind, her steps slowing.

True, many things to this day hadn't been as perfect as she had made them out to be in her fantasy. It wasn't that she expected a lot of praise—she was used to bosses who only ever spoke up if something was wrong. The problem—nothing ever had been wrong. She had never given them an opportunity, until now. She needed to think clearly, to take a moment away from it all.

She couldn't go back to work and pretend this major screw-up had never happened, a few more hours until they'd say the word and send security to escort her out.

Dana wasn't going to wait for it.

She turned on the heels of her expensive boots and walked back into Sheldon's office.

"Dana, I'm sorry, we don't have time for you now," Sheldon junior said, looking slightly irritated. "You'll have to wait until—"

"No. This can't wait. I quit."

He rolled his eyes. Marks sighed, probably dreaming of the drinks by the pool he would have if he hadn't had to come back here.

None of the men looked her in the eye, and none of them tried to dissuade her, which told Dana everything she needed to know. It didn't matter what Peter had or hadn't done. It had never mattered to begin with.

There would be no champagne this weekend, but she might break into one of the bottles of wine they had bought for an upcoming dinner party with friends.

It was that kind of day.

·♥·♥·♥·♥·♥·

In the course of those disastrous events, Dana had forgotten that she didn't have her purse with her. She still couldn't catch Tricia on the phone, and she didn't want to talk to anyone else. The only alternative left was walking. It had begun to snow again, a thin white coat over the icy, dirty mix beneath. Her boots would be put to the test. She didn't even care anymore. On the bright side—once she was home, it would be a more appropriate time for a drink.

Tricia was pretty much free to choose her working hours, and perhaps she could take a break...they could order in...A little TLC and sympathy would go a long way to clear her head.

As much as there was to clear up. Trying to avoid the shoppers with their multiple huge bags, Dana acknowledged that she had been miserable for some time. Getting out of those boots and maybe into a hot bath, a glass of wine, all of those would help with the immediate symptoms. She couldn't deny that her discomfort had been growing for some time, with the clients they were taking on, with the permanent excuses made for Cassidy's behavior. What if she had always been fooling herself, thinking they valued her work? She'd been the token woman in an old boy's club, placed strategically so no one could accuse them of sexism. For the optics. She was sick and tired of it. There had to be something else waiting for her. Somewhere.

She hadn't even managed to think about anyone's Christmas gifts, let alone start buying them. Needless to say, she didn't feel much in the spirit.

That might or might not change once she had the chance to gain a little distance from everything that had happened today, and in the past weeks.

Her feet hurt. She had not expected to take a long walk like this today, but eventually she unlocked the front door of her apartment building, stepped into the lobby and then, the elevator, riding up to the eighteenth floor.

The apartment was quiet when she walked inside. Dana took a moment to lean against the door, taking a deep breath. Home. She took off her boots and put them away, then came back into the living area, frowning at the clothes on the couch. Maybe Tricia had used the time to do some laundry? She picked up one item. Taking a closer look, Dana stared in confusion at the black—and unfamiliar—thong. She refused to let the thought form fully, because on this crappy day, there couldn't be anything else going wrong. It was impossible.

"Tricia! I'm home," she called, quickly dropping the piece of underwear when she realized she'd still been holding it. She went upstairs to the master suite, opening the door softly in case Tricia had decided to take a nap. Which made so much sense in the middle of doing laundry, right?

Only the washing machine wasn't on, and Tricia wasn't taking a nap. She lay under the sheets, curled up with another woman, naked. Dana wasn't sure why she was focusing on the "naked" point. Cuddling and kissing in bed on a snowy afternoon, with someone who wasn't your significant other, could never be harmless.

She was equally unsure about how significant she could still be to Tricia, given the sight in front of her.

"What the hell?"

The other woman jumped and averted her eyes.

"I can't believe this. I can't believe this." Dana said it twice for emphasis and then rushed from the bedroom, slamming the door. It didn't feel as good as she'd thought it would. Forget about the wine, she'd go straight to the vodka. If only to make herself believe, for a little while, that today never happened. She'd wake up in her bed in the morning, get to work on time...

"Damn it."

The bedroom door opened, and the stranger in her home tried to make herself invisible as she all but tiptoed past Dana, coat and keys in hand. Tricia followed, and once the third party was gone, an uncomfortable silence ensued.

Dana wasn't willing to give Tricia an opening. After a few more seconds ticked by, Tricia spoke.

"You're not even going to ask me why? We're not going to talk about this?"

Dana shook her head. "This is rich. As far as I'm concerned, there's nothing to talk about."

"Oh really? You can't think that this is only my fault. But hey, we're not talking about it. What else is new?"

The anger in her voice caught Dana off guard. Was she hallucinating? Was Tricia?

"Wait a minute. The last thing I checked you were in bed with this...woman. Who is she? How long has this been going on?"

"Come on. You can't be that surprised, can you? You basically live at the office, and when you're home, you're always distracted and on call twenty-four seven. I tried to talk to you about it. You didn't listen to me."

"Wait...what? This can't be real."

"Now that it's out in the open, can't we sit down and talk? I don't want to—"

"I don't care. Look, this is what I'm going to do. I'm staying with a friend tonight." Dana hastily took out her cell phone and started writing a text. "When I come back tomorrow morning, I want you out."

Tricia's eyes widened dramatically.

"You don't mean that!"

"You bet I mean that. You might want to start packing."

"Dana." She reached out to touch Dana's arm.

Dana all but jumped back, nearly missing a step. Her cell phone started buzzing, announcing Annie's response. She was one of the friends they were supposed to be celebrating with this weekend.

"Don't touch me. Just...don't."

She hurried back up the stairs and quickly threw various items into the smallest suitcase in the wardrobe—toothbrush, brush, underwear, a change of clothes.

Dana was almost by the front door when she returned to the kitchen and grabbed the bottle of wine she'd been looking forward to. If she was inviting herself to Annie's house, she could at least be a considerate guest.

Tricia observed her actions with an alarmed expression.

"I don't understand you. It didn't mean anything! I just wanted to be close to someone, for once."

"Oh, do you even hear yourself? Goodbye, Tricia. I hope you'll find what you were looking for. I'm sorry that I worked so much that we could live in a nice apartment with a view. Why am I still here?"

A few minutes later, something was going right finally. She caught a cab on the first attempt, and this time, she remembered to take her wallet with her.

Chapter Two

DANA

Annie and her wife Kristen fortunately didn't ask too many questions. Dana showing up with a change of clothes and a bottle of wine shortly before the scheduled celebratory dinner was enough for them to deduce something was wrong.

Dana didn't get the hot bath she'd envisioned, but her friends let her freshen up in the guest bathroom before she was treated to a homemade dinner—including the wine she'd brought, and some from her hosts' fridge.

"I quit my job today," Dana said once she felt safely buzzed, knowing she wouldn't burst into tears.

"Why?" Annie was perplexed. "I thought you were really happy there."

"And I broke up with Tricia."

"Okay, I would lie if I said this was the bigger surprise, but I'm really sorry. You're having one hell of a day."

Dana laughed half-heartedly.

"That's a pretty good way to describe it. Why did everyone see it coming but me? I feel so naïve." So what if she sounded a tad whiny? Everything had gone wrong today. She was entitled to whine, if only for a few hours. Tomorrow would be different. Tomorrow she'd take back control of her life. Probably. Dana drank another sip from her glass. "No, don't answer that. I am—was naïve. I don't know what I was thinking, imagining that they thought I was doing a good job, or that Tricia ever loved me..."

"Oh, honey."

Annie leaned forward to embrace her. "I wasn't going to say it, ever, but I will now. You can do so much better."

"I agree," Kristen said. "The apartment is yours anyway, right?"

"Yes. I guess I have to be grateful that I won't be homeless on top of it all."

"Come on, you know we'd never let that happen, right? And what about that house in the country, can't you rent it out? I'm sure some people would love to go there over the holidays."

Okay, perhaps she didn't have that much reason to whine, but this all seemed too much to think about at the moment. The house had been a steal, since the owners wanted to get out of it quickly. There were times when she had envisioned spending the holidays there with Tricia, now, and in the future. In one of her fantasies, Dana had even gone as far as including children. She was fairly certain that now, it would never happen.

How could she trust anyone, ever again?

There was no point in it. It wasn't worth it. Annie and Kristen were that rare example, the exception to the rule.

"I don't know. I'd have to go up there and see what it looks like. Frankly, we haven't done much with it yet."

Perhaps it had been a tad too rustic for Tricia to begin with, and of course Dana was always working, so they'd put it off.

There was someone in town who looked after it, made sure there were no uninvited guests, and that nothing was falling apart, but that was it. She had bought the house furnished and had gone back once after getting the keys.

"Wouldn't now be a good time?" Kristen wondered. "The sooner you get tenants, the better. You could even make it an *Airbnb*, collect some income while you decide what to do next."

"You still want to practice law, right?" Annie asked.

The realization that she didn't even know the answer to that question for sure was devastating. Dana knew she had to do something, because the next paycheck from Sheldon & Marks would be the last. She could live a while on her savings, but they would run out eventually.

Would anyone even hire her after her impromptu exit? Would the press pounce on the expensive settlement? Panic mode. For a few seconds, she found it hard to breathe.

"Getting out of town might not be such a bad idea."

"Then do it. Clean it up a little, put it up for rent, and go from there. We could even visit you between Christmas and New Year's."

"You don't need to check up on me," Dana protested. She wasn't sure yet whether being alone in the country would be helpful or drive her crazy. A few days in a spa hotel in the city might serve her better, but she had to make some good financial decisions in the coming weeks. She was grateful that her friends could be pragmatic over wine and reassurances. "But it might be fun. I'll talk to the caretaker tomorrow, see when I can go."

"Now that's good news," Annie said. "About the job. This is final?"

"Oh, it is. They were going to fire me this afternoon. The only way I could get out with my dignity intact was to beat them to it, though negotiating a severance package might have been wiser...That, of course, was before I came home to find Tricia in bed with..." The look Annie and Kristen gave each other told her that they hadn't figured out that detail until now.

"It's been the worst day, and I haven't gotten anyone's Christmas presents yet. Do you think we could call it a night?"

"Of course, honey." Annie hugged her again. "Good night. Try to get some sleep. Tomorrow will be better."

Dana didn't say what was on her mind—the bar was extremely low. If tomorrow wasn't better than that, she had no idea what to do with the rest of her life.

·♥·♥·♥·♥·♥·

Alone in the guest bedroom, she cried a little, mostly out of frustration and disbelief. Perhaps it was wrong, but she couldn't make herself feel too broken-hearted over either the job or Tricia, and that in itself was alarming. Worse, though, that for the first time in her life, she had no definitive plan, no idea of what the future would bring, or what she even wanted it to bring...She had to make a living, that much was for sure, even though she was fortunate enough that it wasn't an urgent issue. She could move into a smaller place. Rent out the house, as Kristen and Annie had suggested. The lack of a challenge in her life might drive her crazy at some point, but then again, her challenges had brought her nothing good either. Everything had seemed so easy, maybe too easy. She was sadly ill-equipped to handle a crisis.

Dana was also exhausted, she realized, when all those troubling thoughts couldn't keep her from having the first good night's sleep in months. Annie and Kristen's house was in a quiet neighborhood, and she didn't wake up until nine o'clock. Dana couldn't remember the last time she'd slept until nine o'clock or had felt this rested. After taking a shower and getting dressed, she walked into the kitchen, enticed by the smell of fresh coffee and breakfast delicacies.

"Hey, good morning. Did you sleep well?"

"Well would be the understatement of the year." Dana hid a yawn behind her hand. "It was magical."

She couldn't remember the last time she'd sat down for a real breakfast, without files to study, either. She wasn't sorry for wanting a career and investing in it. It was a sad and bitter realization that she might have invested her energy in the wrong places. Perhaps the insurer had been wrong to deny coverage, and it was a good thing some ultra-rich people hadn't gotten any richer. Where did that leave her?

"That's good. Come sit down, before it gets cold. Annie had to go into work early today, but she'll catch up with you later."

"I'm really grateful for you taking me in." For a split-second, Dana thought about intervening when Kristen filled her plate, but who in their right mind could resist the smell of bacon, eggs, and waffles? She'd pay for her sins at the gym. Dana hated to think Tricia might have some sort of a point, alleging Dana had found time for everything except their relationship. But exercise was important for your health, wasn't it, and cheating was just wrong. "I'll be home later," she continued. "I'll have to pay my debts to a latte-addicted lawyer, and call the caretaker...but first, I think I'm going to eat all of this. I'm weak."

"You're human. That's not the worst thing."

She wasn't going to argue.

·❤·❤·❤·❤·❤·

The first order of business was to catch Rowan before work and pay her debts. Dana had sat in her car, unwilling to go into the building, hoping she wouldn't run into anyone else she knew.

"Thank you for this," Rowan said. "I was serious though. I would have accepted lattes for payment."

Dana didn't tell her that it was unlikely they'd be running into each other soon.

From her car, she made the call to the caretaker.

"Yes, everything is fine, why would you ask?"

Why wouldn't she? She owned the place, and Mr. Toby Griffith was paid to make sure it wasn't robbed or falling apart.

"I'd like to come down for a few days. Could you meet me the day after tomorrow, in the morning?"

"The day after tomorrow? You really want to come before the holidays?"

What difference did it make? Dana was beginning to get irritated with him.

"Yes, that's the plan. Is that a problem for you, Mr. Griffith?"

"Oh no. No problem. I'll meet you there at ten?"

"Yes, please. Thank you."

She wondered what his reluctance meant, but then she remembered that on the few occasions she'd met him, he seemed rather awkward. Well, they didn't need to interact more than necessary, and if she could sell the place soon, he'd never have to deal with her again.

It was a good question. What had possessed her anyway to acquire this house in a somewhat remote village—the idea of romantic vacations with Tricia? Nothing could be further from her mind, or reality in general, right now.

Dana returned to her apartment to find Tricia's side of the closet, and the bathroom, empty. That was what she had asked for, wasn't it? She walked into the kitchen, opened cabinets. Tricia had taken her favorite cups, and a few knickknacks as well. It seemed like a good idea that they'd never gotten around to getting that cat. Dana assumed it would be gone too, and for some reason, the thought made her sad. She really needed to get out.

Dana went to her computer to check out the route. The weather should be fine to drive out for the next couple of days. She hoped the snow wouldn't get too bad in case she needed some more hired work to get the house ready. She welcomed the variety of small tasks, a distraction from the question of whether she'd made a huge mistake. With the job. With Tricia. Should she have groveled more with the partners? Try to see Tricia's side of the story? No. The moment someone cheated, there ceased to be another side. As for the job, she hadn't lied when she told her friends that she would have ended up the scapegoat—no amount of groveling would have saved her.

They were right. If she could sell or rent out the house and make enough money to take a break and reevaluate her priorities, it would be the best possible outcome.

She wondered if she should call her mother, but then decided to wait until she could share some good news as well.

·♥·♥·♥·♥·♥·

The drive would be about five hours, not counting the inner-city traffic. Dana remembered the last time, just a couple of days ago, she'd been stuck in that cab, not knowing that her life would be irreversibly changed hours later.

So far, she was holding up nicely, she thought. Putting things in motion. Being pro-active. There were a couple of firms she could contact, though probably not before the New Year. That would give her plenty of time to wrap up things in Chestnut Hill.

As Dana packed for a few nights' stays, she felt strangely excited. Strange, because she'd said goodbye to everything that had seemed good and predictable in her life. It was kind of ter-

17

rifying—and liberating. She called Annie to inform her about the plans she'd made, and they agreed that Annie and Kristen would come by some time after Christmas.

Six a.m. came quickly. Dana opted for a quick coffee at home. She would stop for a real breakfast later.

She'd wanted an early start, knowing the traffic wouldn't be as bad as later in the day, and true to her hopes, she was soon on her way out of the city. It was beautiful around Christmas. Truth be told, Dana never had much time to enjoy that beauty since she'd moved here, always busy, always chasing something...It was time for a break. She wished Tricia could have talked to her first before deciding she was going to find what she needed outside their relationship.

Maybe it had never been as good as Dana imagined it to be. Maybe she was losing her mind. In any case, she'd have a few days to herself, no immediate deadlines, no arguments, and she'd make that time count.

It occurred to her that she had already made peace with another rushed holiday season, because there was never any time to enjoy dinner parties and Christmas Eve too much. Solitude would do her some good.

Dana was determined to make it come true.

She stopped around nine at a diner hidden away from the highway to have breakfast. Having made good headway, she wasn't nearly as rushed as the people coming and going. This was amazing. There was a life she barely remembered. It was possible she'd never had it, because to achieve and succeed had always been like breathing to her. Learning came to her easily. She didn't have much interest in the usual college antics—and she'd avoided frat parties at all costs—so she'd breezed through. Same with the job.

The job...In retrospect, Dana assumed she should have seen it coming. Sheldon senior's influence was waning, and Cassidy had been tight with the son, from the beginning. Marks didn't care much anymore unless something involved palm trees and golf courses.

Dana sighed as she sipped her coffee. Had she gone at this all wrong? Palm trees didn't sound so bad at all. A week in a resort somewhere South...But she could always do it next year, once everything was settled with the house, and she'd made the final decision whether to rent or sell. She hoped it wouldn't take that long.

"Everything okay, honey?"

Fairly surprised, Dana looked up at the waitress who refilled her coffee cop. *What do you mean? This* is *my hopeful, optimistic face!*

"I'm fine, thank you."

"Anything else I can get you?"

"The check, please." The Good Morning Brunch would carry her all the way to her destination, and if she remembered correctly, there were a bunch of small, charming restaurants in town. She would have time to explore the house by herself, make a list of things to change, and how to get them done, and be ready with her questions for Toby.

Dana paid and left the diner, giving a smile to the woman who held the door open for her on the way out.

Clearly, not all was lost. She'd come back to the city refreshed and able to tackle new challenges. The next year she'd be the best ever version of herself. Promise.

Chapter Three

DANA

A few hours later, Dana stood in front of her property, unsure how she was supposed to react. If she felt like crying again, it might be from the long, fairly exhausting drive. That was at least one explanation—the other could be that her supposed income property was looking a little abandoned. It had snowed here in the past few days, but no one had taken care of it. The shutters needed a fresh coat of paint, and so did the door. She frowned. It hadn't looked like this the last time—or had she seen everything through rose-colored lens? Why had she bought this house in the first place?

True, the surroundings were idyllic. It stood on a small hill that allowed a beautiful view of the town below, that, Dana assumed, would be even more amazing at night. Once she had finished her inspection and to-do lists, she could drive down and take a look around. Later, a nice hot bath, and perhaps she could even light a fire in the wood-burning fireplace...Dana needed some sort of motivation as she realized that her coat and boots were fine for the city winters but didn't quite conquer the cold around here. Just as well—she wouldn't stay that long. Her heels sank deep into the snow as she walked towards the house. The key didn't turn on the first or second attempt. She was shivering hard by the time she opened the door and stepped inside.

It was freezing. Dana shook her head, thinking she'd have to have a stern word with Griffith the next day. He had known she was coming—she would have expected him to take care of it—as defined in his job. Caretaker. Dana put her suitcase aside but kept boots and coat for the moment. She walked around, turning on every heater in the house, increasingly dejected as she took stock. Rustic charm, that's what she'd been sold on. Dana had been so sure she'd find time and ways to modernize the interior and spend many happy hours here...but here she was, alone, and instead of charming, the furniture and décor looked old and outdated.

There was a sharp draft in the bedroom—and another wood burning fireplace. They might have been the reason why she'd been drawn to this property in the first place. Dana couldn't think of much else. She checked the window and realized it wasn't closing properly. On the bright side, if someone had tried to come in, they probably wouldn't have found much worth stealing. There was no money or anything of much value in here. *As for the to-do list—how about everything?* For sure, it wasn't Griffith's fault that she'd had romantic notions about the house and ignored the finer details. The snow, the withering paint, the window, those were things in his job description. At least she had naively assumed so.

After several attempts to close the window, Dana decided she'd sleep in the living room and have Griffith fix the problem ASAP. The fridge was still unplugged. She'd need a while to get it going as well, before she could buy groceries. The kitchen looked fine, equipped with the necessities. Dana sighed in relief when she saw the coffeemaker. There was no coffee to be seen anywhere, but that was an easy fix.

She wandered around a bit more, realizing the temperature in the house hadn't changed a bit. *Please, no.* She couldn't stay here if the heating system was broken as well. What was worse, she might look at a costly repair that would likely delay her plans of getting money out of the house soon. Did that really need to happen on top of everything else? She thought she'd paid her dues already when she came here leaving behind a career and a relationship gone bad.

Dana sat in the breakfast nook, taking in the wet stains her boots had made on the wood floor. She could do this, right? All the house needed was a little TLC, a bit more functionality, and the offers would come. Rushed city dwellers in need of a remote place, ski enthusiasts, families, etc. It was big enough to be comfortable for four, five people. It would rent or sell itself, right? She'd have options.

She stood up to get a pen and notebook and wrote down: *Heating.* She underlined it twice before she added, *fix window, check all windows and doors.* There was a backdoor leading out to a patio, but it was all covered in snow now. In the summer, it would be great to hike around here. Dana took another look at her list and added *paint job.* That was unlikely to happen before the spring.

She called Griffith's number, and almost gave up before he answered on the eighth ring.

"I'm here," he grumbled. "What's the emergency?"

"I think a broken window and no heat qualify."

"Oh, it's you. Ms. Clover."

"Yes, it's me. I'm surprised you didn't check on these things, but I hope you can meet me tomorrow at eight. We have a lot to talk about."

"Eight?" he said, and she could almost hear him frown.

"I'd like to get started early. I need a functioning heating system, and a window that closes in the bedroom. Also, I'd like you to start with the snow removal as soon as possible, oh, and there are a few places outside that need paint. Perhaps you could buy it, and get going as soon as it's warm enough."

Silence.

"Mr. Griffith? Toby? Can you hear me?"

"I hear you fine, Ms. Clover. You must have misunderstood something. I can take a look at that window and the heating, but that's not really my job. I said I'd keep an eye on things, and I did."

"Well, things are falling apart, and it is your job." She took a deep breath, trying not to raise her voice too much. She still needed him. "Look, why don't you come over tomorrow—at nine—and we'll have a coffee, talk this over?" *As the coffeemaker seems to be the only thing that's functioning as it should.*

"Okay then," he said after a moment of hesitation. "I'll be there."

"The paint can wait, but I need you to take care of the other stuff. Bring me someone who can fix the heating if you can't, and the window too. I want that done tomorrow. There's snow in the forecast."

"So I've heard. Thanks for calling. I have to go."

"Of course you do," she said after ending the call. She wouldn't sit around idly either. With renewed determination, Dana got to her feet. She'd drive to town to buy dinner and perhaps a sensible pair of boots. An additional blanket and a space heater might help, too. She'd survive for one night.

Or perhaps...there was something she could try first. How hard could it be? It was probably just the matter of finding a reset button and, well, reset the thing? She vaguely remembered her father doing something similar in one of the houses she'd lived in with her parents. She'd be so embarrassed if she brought in a specialist, when the only thing she had to do was to hit some button...Better find out now and contact Griffith again. Down in the basement, she found a set of tools in a cabinet, and the central heating system. Dana regarded it critically. In most of her adult life, she didn't have time to fix anything—as a consequence, she hadn't learned that much about these things other than when they affected contractual law. Besides, when something broke, she paid someone to fix it. Tricia had been a bit more handy, but not by much. She'd encountered surprise before, because apparently, lesbians were supposed to be able to fix everything. Kristen was working in a garage she part-owned. Ari, one of her friends who was as butch as they came, was one hundred percent on board with Dana's motto—if it's broke, have the number for the emergency service nearby.

But damn it, she'd wasted almost five minutes pondering clichés, and she was still freezing. There was a plan taped to the wall, but most of it was faded. Dana got as far as realizing she'd have to remove the panel to reveal the reset button. So far, so good. She picked up a screwdriver from the toolbox with clammy fingers. Down here, it was even colder. It soon became clear to her that no one had tried to move these screws in a long time. No matter how hard she tried, none of them would budge.

Dana didn't quite know how it happened, but there was no time to avoid disaster between the moment the screwdriver slipped and instead of moving the screw, ended up stabbing her wrist. She stared at the wound in disbelief—how did that happen?

She was almost mesmerized by the blood welling up, a feeling of faint queasiness quickly turning into full blown nausea. Okay, no more fixes. She was going to wait things out until Toby could do his job. At the moment, it was a small consolation that he seemed as clueless as she was, not that it helped much. The only thing it meant was that she'd have to write more checks.

"It never ends," she said out loud.

The wound was pulsing angrily. She'd have to get back up and clean it, bandage it. Now. Dana picked up the screwdriver, letting out a couple of swear words when she realized there was rust on it, likely from the screw. She couldn't remember the last time she'd gotten a tetanus shot. Somehow, none of this was a big surprise. Oh well. She'd wanted to get into town anyway. Dana went back upstairs where she found a lonely, but clean looking towel in the bathroom—that had to do for now. The next neighbor was about twenty minutes on foot away, and she doubted Toby Griffith would be available to drive her. She waited until the nausea passed and went back outside.

·♥·♥·♥·♥·♥·

Dusk was falling when she reached the town, a few snowflakes dancing, the sky still pink from the last rays of the sun. Christmas lights and decorations everywhere.

Dana didn't have much of an eye for the beauty. She still didn't have the clothes she'd intended to buy, and she had to find dinner somewhere. While her stomach had been churning at the sight of the blood earlier, it was growling now, reminding her that the Good Morning Brunch had been a long time ago. She needed to go shopping or find a place to stay overnight, but now all her clothes were up in the house on the hill.

"Oh boy," the pharmacist said when she showed him the wound. "I can bandage it for you, but you might need stitches. What happened?"

"Just what I needed." Dana preferred to avoid an answer to the question. She better not sit in some emergency room for hours. Did they even have a hospital in this town? If she had to drive anywhere, she'd have to raid the vending machine for dinner. So far...not good at all. Perhaps it would have been a better idea to update her résumé and contact those two firms rather than make the rash decision she'd made. Instead of preparing for a rushed, but lovely Christmas in the city, she was alone, hurt, no job, no Tricia, nothing. Nothing except her determination not to break into tears in front of this fairly sympathetic man.

"Okay," she said, averting her gaze when he bandaged the wound. "Where do I go to get those stitches done if necessary? Is there a hospital anywhere close?"

"You're lucky. Dr. McEwen is just across the street."

"Lucky. That sounds good." There was still hope. After all that this was only a small delay. "Thank you so much."

She found the practice after walking across the street and a few steps to the left. Dana opened the door, relieved that at least, she wouldn't be freezing in here.

The waiting area was empty. This could be the beginning of a wonderful lucky streak, right?

"Hi," she said to the receptionist who looked up at her with a friendly smile. "The pharmacist told me I might be able to see the doctor? I had a little accident."

The woman's eyes widened at the blood seeping through the bandage. "Okay, I see...come with me, please."

"Wait, don't you want my insurance information first...?" Dana bit her lip, realizing that she wasn't employed anymore...on the other hand, she was still going to get one last check, which should cover this month, shouldn't it? She felt dizzy again, so she was happy when Ms. Fowler directed her into a treatment room and asked her to sit. "We'll deal with the paperwork later. Dr. McEwen will be right with you."

"Okay." Just as well. "Thank you."

It was definitely much warmer in here. Even hungry and hurting, she didn't mind staying here for a few minutes. Dana closed her eyes, wishing it was already the next day, and she'd have heating, and bought everything she needed to make her stay anything less than a disaster. On the bright side, she wouldn't feel bad at all parting with the place. Selling it still might be the least trouble, even if in its current state. The view alone should guarantee an acceptable price.

Soon enough, she'd be back enjoying the city life, with a new job, perhaps a new apartment, and infinite freedom—single, potentially dating. Never again she'd let too many emotions and expectations get in her way. Annie and Kristen had advised her to think of herself—that's what she was going to do. If she didn't bleed to death first.

Dana jumped when the door opened and a woman in a lab coat walked in. Her auburn hair was rolled up in a neat bun—why did she even notice that?—and she had warm brown eyes. Irritated with herself, Dana said the first thing that came to mind, "Ms. Fowler said she was going to get the doctor?"

The woman smiled. "I am Dr. McEwen."

Her calm matter of fact tone told Dana that she hadn't received that reaction for the first time. Dana could feel her cheeks heat.

"Oh my God, I am the worst. I'm so sorry. In my defense, you look young...and I'm shutting up now. I had an unpleasant run-in with a screwdriver."

"Don't worry about it. Let's take a look."

Dana was happy to let the young doctor be the only one to take a look. She gritted her teeth through the careful examination, fixing her gaze on the calendar on the wall. The house on the December page looked a lot like the one on the hill, romantic with the lights, and snow falling. An illusion. There was nothing romantic about being cold and lonely, no matter what the season was.

"May I ask you what happened?"

"I tried to—" It took her all her self-restraint not to snap at McEwen when she examined the wound.

"Let's say I'm not as good at fixing things as I wish I was. The pharmacist said I might need stitches? I should also tell you that there was a bit of rust on the screwdriver."

"I see. This won't require stitches, but when's the last time you got a tetanus shot?"

Dana wracked her memory. She came up empty.

"Oh, fu—I mean, sorry. I haven't had the best of day...days. As to your question, I don't think I had anything of the kind after sometime in my teenage years." With the new bandage finally in place, she dared to take a look.

"Let's refresh it right now, and you're good to go."

Dana listened to Dr. McEwen explain the vaccine, and all of a sudden felt incredibly tired.

"Great. I still have a lot to do."

"You came to town for work?" the doctor made small talk while she prepared the injection. At the sight of the needle, Dana's stomach did a flip-flop again.

"Oh no. I'll be here over the holidays, in the house on the hill." She didn't think McEwen's question required more context.

"It's a nice place. A bit remote, but it must be beautiful this time of year."

Oh yes, freezing, snowed in and old. She wondered if there was sarcasm in the doctor's tone but couldn't detect any.

"There...almost done. If you could lift your sleeve..."

On the bright side, she didn't have to drop her pants like the last time. That was the only saving grace. Dana hadn't known that the prick of a needle would be the last straw, but all of a sudden, the tears started falling beyond her control.

"You're good. All done."

"I'm so sorry!"

"It's all right. A lot of people have a fear of needles. You're going to be fine."

"No, you don't understand. I quit my job, my girlfriend cheated on me, and I can't even turn on the damn heating without stabbing myself! I'm not fine. Nothing is fine. It's going to be the worst Christmas ever. I wish I could just cancel it."

"Ms. Clover. It sounds like you've had a lot of stress lately. It makes a person a bit of a Grinch, I understand that." McEwen handed her a box of tissues. "I'm sure Mr. Peterson can take a look at your heating system. He's only a couple blocks down the street. I can't do anything about Christmas, I'm afraid, but how about I get you a coffee while you fill out the paperwork?"

Despite herself, Dana managed a smile. "That would be great. Thank you."

"You're welcome. I'll be right back."

Left alone for the moment, Dana tried to process what had just happened. The wound still hurt, none of her problems had been solved yet, but she felt a bit better, if slightly flustered after the small breakdown. She had tried hard to maintain an optimistic attitude, but in one moment, it all came crashing down. She wasn't sure whether she appreciated that it happened in the presence of a sympathetic stranger, or if she was more embarrassed about it. This was not the way she liked to interact with an attractive woman like McEwen. Then again, she wasn't likely to see her again anyway, so why did it matter?

The doctor returned with a clipboard and a cup of coffee.

"I didn't know how you take it...I can get you some milk and sugar if necessary."

"This is perfect, thank you. And I want you to know that I'm not going to scam you out of the money. My insurance should still be covered for this month."

"I didn't think you were going to," McEwen said, and Dana turned her attention to the questions. When she paused, looking up again, she realized the doctor's gaze was still on her.

"Good. You must know your way around town pretty well, right?"

A smile played over her lips. "You could say that."

"I really need to buy some shoes and clothes, and a few blankets. Even better, if you can tell me where I can get wood for the fireplace...I'm afraid my caretaker didn't take his job very seriously."

"You'll find most of that on this street. Except for the wood, of course, you'd have to go a little out of town for that."

"Of course. When I drove out of town, I assumed that everything would be taken care of," Dana said ruefully. "And I didn't think it would be this cold. One last thing...Where could I get some decent food around here?"

"That depends on what you prefer..."

"Frankly, right now, I'd eat whatever anyone wants to put in front of me. I'm sorry, that's not what a doctor wants to hear...I assume." She put the clipboard aside.

Dr. McEwen hesitated for a moment, and Dana almost thought she was going to give her a lecture on the importance of eating well.

"Look, if your shopping can wait another day, I could close up here now and show you a place. Unless you think...I mean...if it's not too straight forward."

Dana thought the doctor was seriously overestimating her at the moment. Her priority was getting food, and soon. She wasn't going to misinterpret an offer from a helpful, friendly townsperson.

"That would be the perfect solution."

Chapter Four

DANA

"I'm just going to show Ms. Clover around a bit. I'll see you tomorrow, Claire."

"Yes, you will," the receptionist confirmed, her curiosity obvious.

For a brief moment, Dana wondered if she'd made a mistake. She'd only be here for a couple of weeks, at the most—no reason to get on the good townspeople's radar for whatever reason. But she felt out of her depth—not to mention, hungry—so she was grateful for the doctor's offer.

They went past a homeware store, and Dr. McEwen halted.

"Your car is here, right? If you want to get a blanket right now, we could go in first?"

"I'll come back tomorrow. I think food is more urgent."

"Yes, of course. Sorry. It's right at the end of the street. Marcie will cook you pretty much whatever you want, but you might want to try her meatloaf. And the apple pie with ice cream is heavenly."

"That recommendation sounds a bit hearty coming from a doctor."

"Oh, believe me, there's a time to indulge yourself, as long as you don't do it every day. Moderation before deprivation, you know?"

"I guess you've convinced me, then."

The interior of Marcie's Café was the perfect picture of a small-town charming diner. No one here seemed rushed, and most of the patrons had to be regulars, judging from the bits and pieces of conversations with waitresses Dana could overhear. The smell of food was enticing, and fortunately, the service wasn't as slow as she had feared.

"Hey, Doc," the waitress, a woman in her mid-thirties, said with a curious look to Dana. "We haven't seen you here in a while."

"Yes, it's been a long time since last week," Dr. McEwen joked good-naturedly. "The usual please."

"And for your friend?"

"I was told that I had to have the meatloaf," Dana said, and she could have sworn the woman's smile got even wider.

"Great choice, honey. What would you like to drink?"

Dana hesitated only a second, unsure whether the doctor might judge her, or why she was constantly seeking her approval anyway.

"I'll have a glass of red wine."

"Water, please." To Dana, she said, "It's been a long day, and you already figured out I'm a chatty person. Wine will make it worse, and I'm not sure you're ready for that."

Dana couldn't help laughing. In the past few days, she'd almost forgotten how good that felt. The warm and cozy atmosphere of her surroundings—and company—presented a vast improvement.

"I'm not so sure. I already had a crying fit five minutes after we met, and you made me coffee. I promise I'll cut you some slack."

The waitress, Lizzie, had approached their table again almost silently, as she brought their drinks. She looked pleased with herself.

"There you go, ladies. You are new in town?" she directed at Dana. "It's beautiful this time of year, isn't it?"

"Why don't we delay the interrogation for a bit?" Dr. McEwen chided.

"I don't mind. It's true that I'm fairly new to Chestnut Hill. I bought the house on the hill, but I haven't been here often since."

"That's a shame. It's a great place, just needs someone to breathe a little life into it."

"Yes, that's the plan."

"Well, best of luck to you. I'll be back with your food soon."

Lizzie cast a triumphant smile at the doctor and walked away.

McEwen sighed when she was out of earshot. "You better get used to it. We have tourists, of course, but other than that, not a lot of new people. Prepared to be the talk of the town for a week or so."

Dana realized that her words held affection rather than irritation. Truth be told, she wasn't used to this much attention from strangers. She definitely preferred their friendly nosiness over Griffith's complete disregard for the task he'd had. But she'd deal with that tomorrow.

"It's fine, really," she said. "And since we're friends now, I'm Dana."

"Holly. Nice to meet you, Dana."

This was absolutely perfect. They would go their separate ways soon enough, but for the time being, Dana was happy to have found someone who had not only catered to her injury but might be helpful in the next few days. She didn't think there was any ulterior motive. Holly was probably married to someone in town—and Dana, after the recent disaster, wasn't looking for anything except good conversation and company either. One could never have too much of that.

Lizzie brought their meals, a delicious looking sandwich with salad on the side for Holly, and meatloaf, potatoes, and vegetables for Dana.

"Oh my God," she said after the first bite. "You didn't exaggerate. This is amazing. Wow."

"It is. Marcie's has been around for over twenty years. Of course, you were hungry and cold for most of the day, but they make great food. There was even a TV crew here for some show a while ago."

"I do understand why." Dana took a sip of her wine, alcohol and curiosity making her bolder than she might have been under different circumstances. "So...we both know why I'm here, but what about you? What made you come to town?"

"Oh, many things." Even though Holly kept her tone light, Dana noticed this might be a touchy subject.

"I'm sorry. I didn't mean to pry."

"No, it's okay. I grew up not far from here. I thought I could make myself useful. Many doctors prefer to get jobs in big prestigious hospitals, but the people in smaller towns need physicians, too."

"That's very considerate."

"I won't lie. I had other reasons, too. And you can't deny it's magical around this time of year. The view from your house must be amazing."

"It is. You could always come by sometime if you like. I'll be dealing with the caretaker tomorrow, and see what else needs to be done, but after that I have nothing else to do. I mean...That sounded bad. If you don't mind coming all the way up, I'd love to have you over."

"Thank you. I'll have to look at my schedule, but that would be nice."

"Yes, absolutely. Doc needs to see other places than her practice or her house sometime," the older woman who had come to their table, said.

"Come on, Marcie, don't be silly. I come here almost every week."

"Sorry, I forgot about that. So, they're actually three places," Marcie said with a wink to Dana. "Can't hurt to add another one. Would you like a coffee with your dessert?"

Dana noticed that there was no question about having dessert, but so far, Holly's recommendation had by far exceeded her expectations.

"Yes please. I hear great things about the apple pie, so that's what I'll go with."

"Me too," Holly said. "Now stop telling embarrassing stories about me, will you?"

"Everyone seems nice around here," Dana observed when they were alone again. "All except for the caretaker, but that's another story." She had more questions, but they would probably cross a line with someone she'd met a couple of hours ago.

"Yes, they are. We're a small community. People stick together."

"In any case...my day is ending on a high note. Thanks so much for bringing me to a warm place—in more than one sense—and getting me fed. I really appreciate it. I can't wait for that apple pie."

"Well, here it is. Enjoy."

"Thanks, Lizzie."

Since Holly had been this helpful, Dana almost asked her if she knew a good real estate agency nearby as well, but she held back the question. Right now, all she wanted was to enjoy the evening, and deal with everything else later. Knowing she might see Holly again would help with the less pleasant tasks of tomorrow, but then again, staying a bit longer might not be such a bad thing.

Her mother—who didn't yet know that Dana had left Sheldon & Marks—would be on her cruise for a little while longer. She'd come to visit Dana in New York in early February. Annie and Kristen had promised to visit, and other than that, Dana had no one else to answer to. If everything went according to plan, she would go home in the New Year, find a satisfactory solution for the house on the hill, and after that, a new job.

It all seemed possible.

It could wait a few days.

She could swear Lizzie was pleased when she took the bill from her.

Holly, however, protested.

"You don't have to do that."

"It's the least I can do after you took care of me. Please, let me."

"All right then. Thank you. But let me pay the next time."

It seemed only natural that there would be a next time. After all, Dana was still finding her way around Chestnut Hill, and there was no one better to keep her from getting lost than Dr. McEwen.

She held the door open for Holly as they stepped outside into the cold, and she was certain that quite a few heads turned.

"They like their doctor," Dana commented. "I can see why."

It was probably only the frigid temperature that made Holly's cheeks redden.

·♥·♥·♥·♥·♥·

The few steps to her car were enough to make her shiver, reminding her uncomfortably of her predicament. Holly had noticed it too.

"You're sure you want to go up?"

"You're right. I should probably go back to that place where they have the blankets and buy a couple. You don't have a space heater you could lend me?" She had meant to make a joke. Holly studied her intently, making Dana a bit flustered.

"Sorry, no. Look...You probably think this is pretty weird, but...I have a small guest apartment with a working heating system. You could stay the night and drive up tomorrow morning."

"What will the people say?" Dana asked jokingly, though she was tempted by the idea. Not because of anything that might make a good rumor. Going back to the freezing house was the least attractive prospect, and perhaps she could do some shopping before going back to meet Griffith.

Holly shrugged. "Whatever they want to. Unless you mind..."

"Hell, no. I can't thank you enough. I swear, I'm usually better at...everything, but a few things have caught me off guard lately."

"I understand. Don't worry about it."

Dana had to admit she was curious about the town doctor, but it seemed Holly's indulgence for said curiosity had come to an end. She took Dana back to the building that housed her practice, and they went up two floors. Perhaps she had hoped for a nightcap, but there was no such offer. Not that she had any reason to complain.

Holly showed her the small, tidy apartment on the top floor while she went around and turned on heaters.

"In a moment, it will be all cozy," she promised. "If you could wait here, I'll bring you some fresh towels and a toothbrush...and there's a coffeemaker in the kitchen."

"This is great, thanks. But I can come down with you and—"

"That's not necessary. I'll be right back."

Okay then. Holly obviously valued her privacy, which was all right with Dana. After all, they had already agreed, more or less, to another dinner, and exploring the view of the house on the hill.

It was such a relief to interact with a person who was genuinely friendly, not because they were trying to get something from you—a commendation, sex, or whatever. In the end, her lack of handiness had led to a lucky coincidence, and she had gotten a tetanus shot on top of it. Perhaps the tide was really turning.

Holly returned a few minutes later, as promised, with a bag that held towels and a packaged toothbrush. She also produced a small bag of coffee, a couple of slices of toast in a ziploc bag, and some jam and butter.

She really didn't want anyone in her space, Dana reflected. Perhaps there was no spouse.

Holly misinterpreted her silence. "If you prefer to have breakfast somewhere else, just leave it, and I'll get it later. It's no problem."

"No, this is perfect. Thanks again."

"You're welcome. Have a good night."

"Thanks, you too. At least now I know frostbite is not in my immediate future."

"Not on my watch," Holly said with a smile, and then she left.

·♥·♥·♥·♥·♥·

Dana woke around eight-thirty, jolted into action at the sight of her watch. The absence of an alarm, and a comfortable, warm place to stay had led to a good night's sleep. Now she had to hurry—after she'd chastised Griffith for all his omissions, being late would undermine her points.

She opted against making coffee as well. Get this over with first, then come back to town for groceries and other errands.

Dana made it back to the house at 8:47 a.m. It was still freezing, even worse so than last night. At least, the fridge was up and running, if still empty. She walked around the house to keep from shivering and took more notes with clammy fingers. Perhaps she had overreacted after a series of mishaps. A good night's sleep had renewed her determination, and Dana found that most changes would be cosmetic, which was a relief.

At 9:14 a.m., there was still no sight of Griffith. Apparently, she had managed to do business with the only person in town that wasn't enthusiastically friendly to strangers. She called, left a message, then called again. This was getting ridiculous.

"Griffith," he finally answered.

"Where are you?"

"Who is that?"

"Dana Clover. I am here at the house on the hill. You said you'd bring someone to check on the heating." Ominous silence followed her words. "You're still there?"

"I can't leave right now. Sorry, lady."

"Hey, sorry isn't going to cut it! You get here right now and bring me someone who can fix the damn heating!" Just like that, her patience had come to an abrupt end.

"Ms. Clover." He laughed as if in disbelief. "I have a job. I can't leave."

"You had no problem taking my money."

"And I did the job you paid me for. I'm not your handyman."

"Mr. Griffith! I could sue you—"

He didn't seem to care much about the prospect, because he hung up on her.

Chapter Five

HOLLY

Claire had brought in the patient files, and she was fidgeting. Holly was well aware of what was on her mind, and Marcie's, and Lizzie's. She wasn't going to make it too easy on any of them. She settled behind her desk and started looking at her schedule for the day, aware that Claire was still standing in the doorway. At this rate, she'd stay there all day.

Holly sighed.

"Is there anything else?"

"Did Ms. Clover find everything she needed last night?" Straight to the point. At least, Claire didn't waste any time. This should be quick and easy.

"You went to Marcie's for breakfast today?"

"I did, but that has nothing to do with it. You had a nice evening, everyone's happy for you, you know that."

Closing the file, Holly shook her head.

"I love you all, but this is not the big deal you think it is. I was trying to be helpful. It looks like someone scammed her, and she doesn't know anyone in town. I wanted to make sure she didn't think everyone behaved the same way."

"So you took her home." Claire smiled.

"You are impossible. She stayed in the guest apartment! The heating at her place is broken. I'd be a terrible doctor if I'd let her stay there."

"Well, perhaps that's the problem. You only think about others' well-being. It's time you took care of your own as well."

They heard the door, and Holly got to her feet.

"Thanks for the advice. I think that's Mrs. Beck. You can tell her to come in."

Claire looked serious all of a sudden. "I'm really sorry if I, if we overstepped, but Holly...it's been three years."

"I'm aware how long it's been. Now, if you could please...?"

"Sure."

Holly made sure her focus was on her patients, and not on those ridiculous insinuations. Mrs. Beck had recently needed an adjustment to her blood pressure medication, but fortunately she was doing fine today. The latest test results had shown the medication was working. However, when Mrs. Beck started talking about her granddaughter's success in culinary school "in the big city," Holly's attention began to waver.

She knew Claire meant well, and so did Marcie and Lizzie, and just about everyone she knew in town—which was almost everyone who permanently lived in town. But Holly didn't need them, or anyone, to give her life a new purpose and direction. She had purpose caring for her patients, and she wasn't crying herself to sleep every night. Not anymore. The practice, and the people who came to see her every day, and the ones who greeted her on the street because she had patched up their kids and helped their loved ones—that was enough. It had to be.

Whatever the town grapevine might make of it, there hadn't been ulterior motives in any of the offers she'd made to Dana

Clover. Holly wasn't looking for fun, though she had enjoyed Dana's company the other night. Perhaps a bit too much...Holly admitted to herself that she'd been a little spooked by the turn of events, her own actions. But she had done nothing wrong or out of the ordinary, keeping her private space private. She might or might not take Dana up on her offer to check out the beautiful view from her house.

She hadn't even realized she'd sighed, until Mrs. Beck asked, "Holly, are you okay?"

"Yes. Mrs. Beck. Don't worry. And that's great about your granddaughter. She will be an amazing chef, no doubt."

The woman's face lit up. "She always loved to spend time in the kitchen. I wish her mother could have seen it."

"She'd be extremely proud."

What was wrong with her? Holly always listened, and she always cared, but it seemed that this morning, she had a hard time hearing just one more sad story—and Mrs. Beck was only the first patient today. It had to be the holidays, just around the corner. Of course, she had a standing invitation from the Crawford family, and she'd stop by for some coffee and pie, but she could never bring herself to attend the family party. Holly always had an excuse—people got sick during Christmas too. Some had a hard time during this period, which was the most joyful of all for others. She often kept the practice open. Some physical symptoms could be caused by anxiety, worries, and fear. Loneliness. But Holly wasn't lonely. She wasn't going to let anyone think she was.

Mr. Resnick was next on her schedule. Holly checked her watch, realizing he was late—which was strange, because the thirty-four-year-old bank employee was always right on the clock. He was trying to quit smoking.

After knocking on her door, Claire came inside. "Mr. Resnick just called. He's very sorry, but he won't make it."

45

"Anyone in the waiting room?"

"Mr. and Mrs. Johnson for the flu vaccine."

"Okay, give me a couple of minutes, then you can send them in."

Holly hoped that between that and the next scheduled appointment, she might be able to head over to Marcie's quickly and get a coffee to go. She felt quite off this morning. With a little luck, caffeine would chase the fog away. She couldn't get sick. There was too much to do.

Fortunately, it looked like she'd make it, Holly realized checking the waiting room a few minutes later. When she shared her plans with Claire, her trusted receptionist jumped to her feet.

"I can go get it." She sounded apologetic.

"No, thanks. I could bring you something though."

"In that case, I'll have one of those chocolate cream cheese muffins. Thank you. And Holly..."

"It's okay," Holly said with a dismissive gesture. "Let's just leave it at that."

As she headed across the street, she was overly aware of the Christmas decorations in every window. Claire usually brought a small artificial tree they kept in her corner of the practice, and they put a wreath on the door, but that was it. Holly didn't decorate at home. As she'd told Dana, she could sympathize with anyone who didn't participate in the extreme merriness. Sometimes, merriness was too hard to deal with. Life changed. It wasn't what she needed or wanted in her life right now.

As Holly placed her order, she was surprised to see Dana sitting at one of the tables, nursing a hot chocolate. For a split-second, she was pleased, bewildered by the sentiment, until she realized that the other woman didn't look happy.

She couldn't stay away, could she? That was just her, Holly McEwen, taking care of everyone before herself. Well, she didn't need all that much. Low maintenance, if you will.

46

"Hi, Dana. Good morning."

Dana looked up at her, a smile lighting up her face.

"Doctor...Holly."

Given the situation, Holly suppressed the smile, thinking that her tiniest patients called her by that name, *Doctor Holly*. In Dana's case, however, it seemed more like an uncertainty of how to address her. Yes, last night had been strange. Strangely comforting.

"Thanks again for letting me stay," Dana said. "I'm afraid it's not a great morning...the caretaker quit on me, and the house is still one giant freezer. Right now, I'm indulging myself, but I'm seriously considering leaving today. This is unacceptable."

"But you can't go before I get the chance to pay for dinner."

She had meant it as a joke, but Holly noticed with some alarm that she was disappointed at the thought of Dana leaving so soon. As much as she loved her surroundings, and was grateful for the life she had, Holly realized she'd appreciated spending some time with an "outsider." Straying off the beaten path for a bit.

"Well, I'm afraid it would have to be tonight. I'm sorry I couldn't present you with the view, but I think this isn't working out."

"Give it a couple of days, maybe? You really should talk to Mr. Peterson. He's right on the corner."

"Yeah. I might do that," Dana said with a sigh. "Again, I can't thank you enough, for your help, and for introducing me to this place. I'm beginning to think everything they make here is heavenly."

Holly saw Marcie standing behind the counter, smiling. She refrained from rolling her eyes.

"It is. Look, I need to head back, but how about you come see me at about seven-thirty, and..." She raised her voice a fraction.

"We'll go somewhere more private." Although, that might have an effect opposite to what she'd desired.

"Sounds great. But you don't have to pay."

"You didn't even have breakfast this morning. Let me."

"All right then. This day is already so much better. I'll see you later, Holly."

"See you."

She had spent a little longer than intended, so she was slightly out of breath when she returned. Jake Connelly was sitting in the waiting room, the image of a flu-stricken patient. Holly handed both her coffee and the muffin to Claire and went back to work. She had an idea, though. After sending Jake home with prescriptions and advice, she picked up the phone. Jake was working for a farmer who sold firewood. This could definitely help with Dana's problem. Holly picked up the phone and called the McKenzie farm.

"Holly, hi, how are you?" Mrs. McKenzie asked.

"I'm great, thanks. Listen, I was wondering if you could make a delivery for me, bring some chopped firewood to the house on the hill? For a couple of weeks or so, just to get started."

She wasn't sure if Dana wanted to use the fireplace on a regular basis, but that way, she'd be able to start heating the place at least, in case the repairs to the system would take longer.

"The house on the hill? I thought that one was empty?"

"It's been for a while, but the owner just came back. It looks like she has some trouble with the heating. Just put it on my bill."

"No problem, I'll tell Patrick to go right away."

"Thanks. That's wonderful."

"That lady, she's a friend of yours?"

For a moment, Holly intended to correct the record, but then she thought otherwise. She might be. A friend.

"You could say that. She's not used to the country life."

Mrs. McKenzie laughed. "I see what you mean. We're happy to help."

That important task taken care of, Holly went back to work. She hoped her surprise would be welcome.

For the rest of the day, she allowed herself no more distractions, up to that moment when she stood in her bedroom after a long hot shower, about to get dressed. The fact that she'd stayed under the spray long enough for the skin on her fingers to wrinkle, definitely had to do with stalling.

A part of her wanted to pull out one of those dresses she hadn't worn in years. Another told her without reservation that this was a silly, stupid idea. She wasn't going on a date. Friends. That was what she was hoping for, and even that was a reach. At best, Dana would spend the holidays, perhaps a few weeks to lay low until she found a new job, and a new girlfriend. Maybe she'd even come back once in a while. There was no reason to over-think this evening and whatever implications it might have.

Holly frowned at her mirror image. It might be that the friendly nagging she'd been exposed to, especially in the last few months, had taken its toll.

No.

She wasn't going to start believing what her nice neighbors kept telling her, more or less between the lines. Things were all right the way they were. She was going out to dinner. Holly took a grey sweater and a black pair of pants out of the closet and started to dress. That was more appropriate.

Half an hour later, Holly suppressed a sigh of relief when she opened the door to Dana. She had changed, too, but like Holly's, her clothes were sensible and casual. Holly noticed that she was wearing a different coat and boots.

"I see you got around to doing some shopping. Does that mean you're staying?"

"Well, I can't leave now. Someone left a mountain of firewood for me."

For some reason, Dana's smile made her blush. There was no hidden meaning to any of her actions. She had learned that if you could do something to help another person, you better do it now. Blink, miss the moment, it could be too late.

"I hope I didn't impose. I thought you might need an option."

"I might need someone who can start a fire," Dana said, amused. "But thank you. I had Mr. Peterson come by as well, and guess what, the house is finally thawing. No doubt this was a bit of a rocky start, but things are so much better now. Mostly, because of you."

At this point, her face was burning.

"I'm glad I could help."

"You definitely did. How much do I owe you for the wood?"

"Nothing. Let's say it's your Welcome to Chestnut Hill gift."

"Then I'm paying tonight, and I won't accept any objections. Where are we going?"

"You like Italian? *La Dolce Vita* is quite nice, authentic, and they are friendly, but not quite as nosy."

"Sounds great. Let's go."

Dana seemed to hesitate, and for a moment, Holly was almost afraid she might try to hug her. Then she was disappointed she didn't.

Chapter Six

HOLLY

The Morelli family had opened their restaurant *La Dolce Vita* a couple of years ago and had been welcomed into the community. Holly had gone a few times, but she didn't have any specific, highly emotional memories connected with the place. That made it perfect.

Holly had no illusions. Everyone in Chestnut Hill who cared to find out that Dana had stayed at her guest apartment, and that she was meeting her for dinner the second time in so many days, would find out. It didn't matter.

She found it a relief to spend time with someone who was trying her best to avoid all things celebratory and merry as well. It wasn't something Holly could address with many people in town. This wasn't just a show the people put up for tourism. They truly loved it. Once upon a time, Holly had, too, but those days were gone.

Caterina Morelli, the couple's daughter, greeted them and saw them to their table, a booth in a cozy corner by the window from which they could see the snow falling softly.

This time of year was tough—even though her workload didn't, time seemed to slow down.

"Is everything okay?" Dana asked, and Holly shook herself out of her reverie.

"Yes, sorry, I was just thinking about a patient. Tell me about your day. I'm glad you finally have a warm place."

"Me too, you have no idea. I'm so happy to talk to people who know what they're doing. Stabbing myself with that screwdriver was the best that could happen to me."

Holly chuckled. "I wouldn't go that far."

"Well, I would. You turned it all around for me." After a small pause, Dana continued. "I'm sorry if that sounds melodramatic, but somehow it seems to fit. My life has been a soap opera this past week."

After Caterina had brought their drinks and taken their orders, Holly asked, "Did you love her?"

Strangely enough, Dana didn't seem to mind the intimate question. She pondered it for a moment, too long, Holly thought.

"I thought I did. I'm still angry that she did that to me. I worked a lot, we barely saw each other, I get that. It's no excuse."

"I agree. You think you could forgive her?"

"I think she's moved on. She hasn't tried to reach me since I kicked her out, and I guess that's the best possible outcome for the both of us."

Holly could tell her own stories about the "best possible out-come" after life took a sharp, terrible turn to the worst. There was an advantage to betrayal. A way to place the blame. To move on.

BELLS WILL BE RINGING

"But please, let's not talk about me all the time. You're married? Single, seeing someone?"

Holly had expected to face these kinds of questions at some point. She had to admit she didn't expect them so soon, and she wasn't ready.

"And that was completely uncalled for," Dana said. "Just because I blurted out my complete relationship drama, basically the moment I saw you, doesn't mean you have to tell me yours."

Her apology gave Holly time to compose herself. Compose an answer, too.

"That's okay. I'm single. Not dating anyone."

"The practice keeps you busy, I assume."

"Yeah, that too. So, what are your plans for the next few days?"

Dana's expression told her that she was well aware of her evasive tactics. She played along.

"Actually...I'm not sure. I can't remember the last time I had so many days off in a row. There's no TV up in the house either. It would be a great time to completely unplug. Perhaps the only opportunity I'll get in some time."

"You'll be looking for a new job?"

"Yeah. I can wing it for a bit, but eventually, I'm going to need some cash coming in."

"You could always rent out the house."

"I could."

"And if you need a place to get away, you just use it for yourself," Holly reasoned.

"Look at you, helping me out again. What did I ever do before I met you?"

Holly was about to apologize again, but she realized that Dana was teasing her. She wasn't sure how to feel about it. Developing a friendship, spending time together, good wine and conversations, that was going to serve them both. Neither of them was ready for anything else, especially with someone they'd just met. Against all reason, she found herself hoping that Dana would put off the job search for a while. In her presence she felt...calm. Safe.

Where did that come from?

"I hope you don't think I'm out of line. Apparently, I don't get enough human interaction outside of the job."

"It's all good. I think I can relate. We just have to be patient with each other."

"I can do that," Holly said, amazed at the warm, pleasant sensation that had nothing to do with the wine, if she was honest. Friendship was good. Important. She wanted Dana to be her friend. It seemed like an achievable goal.

"Good." If Dana wanted to say anything else on that subject, she kept it to herself when their food arrived, pizza baked in the traditional stone oven. "Wow, this looks amazing. You want to try a piece of mine?"

"Only if you have a piece of mine."

It took some wriggling, but eventually they managed. Nothing to see here, Holly thought. It's what friends did, sharing a meal and a nice glass of Chianti by candlelight.

She hadn't felt this alive in a long time.

She'd really needed a friend.

·♥·♥·♥·♥·♥·

Dana did hug her that night, so quickly Holly could have almost fooled herself into thinking it didn't happen. She caught a whiff of her perfume, her hair soft against Holly's cheek.

"Thanks for another great night," Dana said. "I know you have work to do, but if you want to check the view some time, like we said, feel free to come back any time. I'll give you my number, but I don't think I'll go out that much now that I have everything I need." She took a card out of her purse and regarded it wistfully before she wrote the number on the back. "I guess they're still good for something. Do you believe things happen for a reason?"

"No," Holly said. "I believe you continue to roll with the punches. Eventually you get good at it...and sometimes, there's even a nice surprise."

"I guess I know what you mean. Good night, Holly. Please, call me sometime."

"I will. Good night."

·♥·♥·♥·♥·♥·

Holly was used to her weeks flying by, especially during this time of year when people were most stressed, flu-stricken or in danger of breaking a limb in ice and snow. This week was different. The reason might be that she couldn't wait for Sunday afternoon to arrive.

She had always thrived on the many different stories, the interactions with her patients, ways to improve their lives beyond the necessary intervention. Holly still did, but she also realized she was tired. It was a strange mix of emotions, in combination with the anticipation of seeing Dana again.

Her last appointment for the day was Kelly Manning who was accompanied by her husband Blake. They had a two-year-old son, and were expecting again, this time, a girl.

"Everything looks great," Holly told them after she'd finished her exam.

"That will be quite a way to ring in the New Year," Blake said, and Kelly smiled at him with an affectionate eye roll. She was glowing. The two were obviously in love and had been when she first met them. When everything was still so raw, she had struggled to make it through the day, but known that if anything could save her, it was this, her profession, her vocation.

Holly owed everything to being a doctor, and the people who had believed she still could be after the worst-case scenario. She knew who she was—and what she wanted.

Didn't she?

After closing up for the day, she went over to Marcie's, faintly disappointed when she didn't see Dana. Which was silly, because they'd made a date (not a *date*) for Sunday. Lizzie came to her table, lingering even after Holly had placed her order.

"Is there something you'd like to ask me? Then please do it now. I'm hungry."

"Why so cranky? Didn't you go out twice with your new friend last week?"

With the weekend getting closer, Holly had been in a fairly good mood, but she was about to get cranky for real. Whether the reason was hunger, or the constant friendly invasion of her privacy, she wasn't sure.

"Please. My sandwich."

"On it." Lizzie laughed. "When are you seeing her again?"

"None of your business...and it's not what you think...Come on, get me my food already."

Amused, Lizzie walked away.

Holly shook her head. They were all so wrong. Yes, she had enjoyed the hug. She liked Dana, talking to her, being with her, but she wasn't after whatever the friendly townsfolk imagined. There was no way anyone or anything could ever compare to the life she'd once had—or thought she had—the one she had imagined. If she knew that already, why try?

And, of course, Lizzie, Marcie and the others didn't know the whole story, Dana's side, the betrayal she'd faced. Neither of them needed adventures and games.

"Good evening, Dr. McEwen."

She smiled back as the McKenzies passed her by.

Mrs. McKenzie stopped by her table. "I hear Peterson finally fixed the heating for your friend, but I think she appreciated the gift. Those logs make for a nice romantic fire, especially this time of year."

Holly suppressed a sigh. "I imagine they do. Thank you for the quick delivery."

"No problem. Whatever you need." She went to join her husband.

Holly leaned back in her seat, thinking that she hadn't talked to Maddy Crawford in too long. What if this year, against all odds, she took her up on her offer to join the family for Christmas? Maddy had told her time and again that she did belong.

She wondered if some of the town's grapevine had reached her already, then decided it was rather a matter of how long ago it happened. There were no secrets in Chestnut Hill. If she ever changed her mind, Holly thought Maddy would be the first who deserved to know. But there was nothing to tell. She'd made a new friend. End of story.

Lizzie brought her meal, and Holly tried to do what she'd always done, go through the week in her head, remind herself why she was here, what the reason for all of this was.

Perhaps she should talk to Maddy, just in case. In the past, that had always helped her when she desperately needed perspective.

Holly wasn't desperate at the moment, just...pensive. The past few days had interrupted her routine in ways she hadn't expected.

· ♥ · ♥ · ♥ · ♥ · ♥ ·

At home, Holly picked up the phone but deleted the number midway. Not yet. Maybe not ever. Maddy Crawford had spent her whole life in Chestnut Hill, the last eighteen as mayor. She knew the town and its people better than anyone else, and she'd be able to distinguish between truth and a benevolent rumor.

No reason to say yes to the Christmas party yet.

Strange to think that none of this would have happened if it weren't for the recent mishaps in Dana's life. If she'd been back in the city, with a fulfilling job and a dedicated girlfriend...then what?

Holly would admit to one thing—she was thinking about her far too much. Her friends might be right—she needed to get out more. Or perhaps she'd try to find out what Dana's plans for the near future were. Somehow, Holly had a hard time thinking she might want to live permanently in Chestnut Hill, even if there was a way for her to find work.

Somehow, that bothered her.

·♥·♥·♥·♥·♥·

The drive up to the house on the hill was a picturesque one, a small but steady climb on quiet streets, along snow-covered fields and trees. Dana had asked her to come around in the afternoon. The sky was already starting to darken some, but it would be later that they'd be able to take advantage of the full view of the city in Christmas lights. It made her think of Whoville. Holly had to smile. She wondered if Dana was warming up to the Christmas spirit.

The more she thought about it, the more it seemed like she might be able to get through a party at the Crawfords' without a crying fit, but there was something holding her back. Dana would be staying during the holidays. Perhaps she was getting ahead of herself, and she'd be fine alone up here.

Holly walked up the steps to the porch and knocked on the door.

Dana must have been close to the door because she opened right away.

"Right on time. Come on in."

Holly stepped inside, halting to let Dana take her coat before she walked into the living room. It was toasty warm, and to her surprise, a fire was flickering in the fireplace. She'd always liked the scent, never lived in a house with a fireplace. The house on the hill was on the rustic side, but it was easy to detect the little changes Dana had made.

"Feel free to take a look around," Dana said. "It's not as bad as I first thought. Mr. Peterson says it has good bones, so I went around town to shop for some knickknacks and kitchen stuff."

There was a coffeemaker, a toaster and a...stand mixer? This made Holly ridiculously happy.

"So, you intend to stay for a while?"

"I guess I went a little overboard, but I really felt like baking a cake. I don't know when I did it the last time."

"Should I be worried?"

"Of course not. I'm just that good."

There was a pause in which Holly wondered if Dana might be flirting with her regardless of the fact that she just broke up with her girlfriend under unpleasant circumstances. And if she had, was it on Holly to put the brakes on, tell her...what? That it felt good to be noticed by an attractive woman? It wasn't that people overlooked her all the time—in fact, her position in Chestnut Hill was a pretty prominent one, both due to her profession, and her association with the Crawford family.

"I have to trust you, then."

"Yes, you do. But sit down first. Can I get you something to drink? A Martini to warm you up, maybe?"

It was Holly's first instinct to decline, but then she thought twice about it. Everything was set up with St. Christopher's hospital in case of an emergency. She'd reopen the practice to-morrow morning. What bad could happen?

"Sure, why not?"

She realized Dana had even put up some Christmas decorations, a wreath with lights. Holly glanced after her as she went into the kitchen to prepare the cocktails.

"You decided not to be a Grinch after all?"

Dana laughed softly. "Guess what, I might even put up a tree. I've realized that I already got a few gifts, even if some of them came in disguise."

"Really?"

Dana balanced the glasses and a couple of plates with cheese, bread, and snacks on a tray. "There you go. And I'm serious. I was uneasy about the case for so long, and to be honest, it wasn't the first. My relationship...I don't want to bore you with that. I guess we weren't right for each other, and neither of us had the courage to say it out loud, so it's better that way. It all made me realize I needed to come here and take care of the house...and I found you."

Quite the find.

"I'm sorry you got hurt, but I'm glad you came to me."

"Well, it's not a big town. We might have run into each other anyway...at Marcie's, for example. But tell me about your week. I bet it was more interesting than shopping for decorations and actually putting up some."

Interesting, it was, Holly thought. *And I've been thinking about you far more than I should.*

"I can't tell you any details, but, you know, people tell me a lot of things. If you're looking for a renter, I could put out the word."

"Maybe." To her surprise, Dana hesitated. What did that mean?

In the following silence, Holly got up, drink in hand, and walked to the big window, taking in the panoramic view of the town in the valley below.

"I didn't oversell it, did I?" She hadn't realized Dana was right behind her, and almost spilled her drink.

"Oh, no way. It's amazing."

"If you're brave enough, we could take a walk after dinner. What am I saying?" Dana laughed. "You're a doctor. Of course you're brave. I swear I didn't mean for it to sound this stupid."

Holly turned to her with a smile.

"I'd love to take a walk with you."

·♥·♥·♥·♥·♥·

"Have you always wanted to live here?" Dana asked after serving dinner—chicken, rice and vegetables with a delicious gravy, and a red wine. "I went away for college, and I studied abroad for a few semesters," Holly said. "I came back to work at St. Christopher's, and when Dr. Shepherd retired, I had the chance to take over the practice, so I did." Of course, she'd left out big parts of the story, why she had chosen to stay in Chestnut Hill in the first place, and why she almost ran, because nothing in her life seemed to make sense anymore. Because she'd thought there was nothing left.

"And you? The big city was always home?"

"I grew up in New Jersey and Vermont," Dana explained. "The first lawyers I knew were in books and TV shows, and they were heroes to me. I guess that's what I wanted to be...and I lost track. I haven't done much for the underprivileged lately."

"But now you have the chance to turn everything around...if you want to."

A job, a career, it was different. Some chances were just gone, forever.

"Yeah, I guess I have to figure out what I want. I know I'm ready for a change, but I'm not sure what exactly that would look like. Some more?" Dana asked, lifting the bottle of wine.

"Oh, no, I shouldn't." It was the right thing to say, even if what Holly wanted at the moment, was the opposite. To let go a little, take a risk, see what would happen. Dana had no idea. She wasn't that courageous. There was a reason why she had hidden in her practice for three years. Once you took that risk, you could get hurt. Badly.

Dana set down the bottle. "Whatever you're more comfortable with. I was thinking, though, if you'd like to stay, I could drive you to town tomorrow morning. I have an early appointment, and you said you're not on call tonight?"

Her face was burning. It might be the fire, the wine, or the implications. No, that was her own runaway imagination. Dana didn't mean it that way. Holly blamed Lizzie and Marcie, and the McKenzies, above all, for their constant insinuations that she and Dana might become more than friends.

"I'm not. Okay. One more sip."

"Let me just clear the table, and we can sit over there." Dana indicated the couch closer to the fire. "No helping. I got this."

True to her word, she was back in a matter of minutes, setting her own glass on the coffee table.

"So, have you decided? There's a guest bedroom down the hall, all set up." She took a look over her shoulder outside. "And it's starting to snow again. Truth be told, I don't feel like a walk that much. We could just stay inside...and relax." Dana shook her head, a bit self-conscious. "This is such a new concept. I have to admit, I really like it."

Holly liked it too. Dana put her arm on the back of the couch, almost around her. Would now be a good time to warn her not to get her hopes up too high? Was Holly flattering herself?

She realized she'd passed the point of no return when Dana leaned in to kiss her, and for a sweet, surreal moment, Holly kissed her back.

Then the guilt kicked in.

What was happening? She'd been on a couple of dates before, pushed by well-meaning friends, knowing they'd lead nowhere. This...it wasn't even a date. Or perhaps she'd been fooling herself into thinking it wasn't.

She pulled back abruptly, feeling even guiltier at Dana's confused expression.

"I'm sorry, I—I can't."

"Can we talk? I'm sorry too...If you think this is some kind of rebound thing for me. It's not. I like you."

If only it had been this easy.

"I like you too." At least, this was honest. Holly wasn't sure how to proceed without sounding melodramatic or opening the door to the pain she'd successfully held at bay for so long. She couldn't go there again. "But this isn't going to happen. I'm sorry if I made you believe otherwise. I better go." She got up to realize the wonderful view she'd come here for—or so she'd made herself believe—was completely obstructed by dense snowfall. She could barely see her car.

"I don't want you to be uncomfortable," Dana said wistfully. "But it doesn't look like you're going anywhere. I swear, I'll behave, and I can still drive you tomorrow."

"I'm not worried about me. I just...I can't talk about it."

"It's fine. Let's take a breath, and I think it's time for coffee and dessert."

Chapter Seven

DANA

For the past week, Dana had felt like she was living in an alternate universe, making herself at home in Chestnut Hill, dreaming about the upcoming evening with Holly...Life had taken an even more surreal turn, and she was grateful for the mundane task of preparing coffee in the kitchen.

She'd thought this meant something. She had even baked a cake.

Dana hadn't baked a cake since her late twenties.

She hadn't lied about her intentions either. This week had given Dana a lot to think about, and she couldn't deny that she and Tricia had lived parallel lives rather than sharing one another's. Finding out about her affair, and the way it happened, had hurt her ego more than anything, but now she was free, to become the better self she wanted to be.

What had she overlooked? Holly seemed so confident, so capable, but what was behind the obvious? Someone had to have hurt her, for her to withdraw so abruptly and completely.

Dana wished she could confront that person. What else could there be? Sure, with their different professions and obligations, it wouldn't be easy to make logistics work, but they could see each other on the weekend, for starters.

But that wasn't what Holly wanted, apparently, and she couldn't tell her why.

Dana smiled wryly. Of course, perhaps Holly wasn't attracted to her. Had she misread the signs so badly? No.

Then again, she hadn't been much aware of her deteriorating work situation, and the fact that her girlfriend was cheating on her.

She carried the coffee cups and cake into the living room. Holly looked pensive. Dana didn't want the atmosphere to be tense and awkward, but she wasn't sure how to avoid it either.

After what seemed like the longest stretch of silence, she said, "Please know I'm not going to push, but if there's something you want to tell me, I'll be here. That's all."

Holly's smile didn't quite reach her eyes.

"I appreciate that. And I have to admit that I'm really curious about that cake."

It wasn't much of a consolation to Dana that it had turned out great.

· ❤ · ❤ · ❤ · ❤ · ❤ ·

Holly turned down breakfast, so Dana decided to drive her first and settle in at Marcie's café for the morning, trying to come up with a plan. She still couldn't make sense of what had happened last night. She wasn't going to break her promise, but she wasn't going to let it go either. Her mind kept lingering on that kiss.

"I'm really sorry, but I need to get going. I'll call you."

"Will you?" The words were out before Dana could stop herself.

"Yes, of course. You have a good day. Thanks for everything."

"You too. I'll see you."

Dana sat in the car for a few minutes after Holly had disappeared into her practice, then she went over to Marcie's where she sat in a booth by the window.

"Hey, what's with the frown?" Lizzie asked. "Christmas is less than a week away."

"Yeah." Dana sighed. "How about you get me one of those blueberry muffins?" She could have had the leftover cake for breakfast, but she'd felt more like being alone among people. "And a latte, please."

"Coming right up." Lizzie looked like she was going to say more, but apparently, she thought twice about it, turned on her heel and left. Between appointments and shopping, Dana had spent a substantial amount of time at the café. She knew that Holly had too, for many years.

When the waitress returned with her order, she asked, "Could you sit with me for a second?"

She wasn't going to invade Holly's privacy, just...interview a witness.

With a knowing smile, Lizzie sat across from her.

"You're asking me what to get Holly for Christmas?"

This was almost too easy.

"Not quite, but this is a good start. What should I get her?"

"You know that she's a big supporter of the local community. A piece of art from one of the galleries...or you could always go with jewelry."

"That's jumping the gun a bit, isn't it?"

Lizzie studied her for a moment. "This isn't about a present, is it?"

"No. I don't know how to say it. I really like her. I got the impression she felt the same..." This was crazy, discussing such private details with a woman she barely knew—regarding a woman she barely knew, a short time after breaking up with Tricia. But this was what mattered right now, above everything else, finding out if she had a chance with Holly.

"Then what's the problem?"

"I don't know, that's the problem. I thought she was interested, and then...I shouldn't be talking to you about this. Let's go back to the Christmas present."

"Wait, you don't know, do you?" Lizzie's eyes widened.

"I don't know what?" Dana returned, alarmed.

"Oh, honey, it's not a secret. We all want Holly to be happy, but you're probably right to take it slow. She lost her girlfriend three years ago."

"Lost?"

"She died, very suddenly, some kind of heart disease that had gone undetected. They were close. Everyone thought they were going to be together forever."

"Oh no. I feel so stupid right now."

"Don't," Lizzie advised. "It's important to grieve, but it's also important to live. Sometimes, life gives you second chances."

Dana wasn't in the mood for daily affirmations, but at least she managed enough politeness not to say it out loud.

"I guess. And sometimes we have to let it go. If she had wanted me to know, she would have told me."

"Louanne was Mayor Crawford's niece. I don't know why she thought you wouldn't find out anyway. It's a small world here in Chestnut Hill."

"Well, I think that was her decision to make."

Now what? Pretend she could go back to NYC, find a new job and apartment, and pretend none of this ever happened?

"I'm just saying, in the past three years I haven't seen Holly take a woman to *La Dolce Vita* or have anyone stay at her apartment. And for sure I haven't seen her smile as much as in the past few days. I hope, for her, that it means something."

"Thanks so much, Lizzie. If you'll excuse me now...I have a lot to think about."

"No kidding, but talk to her. Soon."

"Don't worry, I will."

What she was going to say, Dana had no idea.

·♥·♥·♥·♥·♥·

After breakfast, she wandered around town rather aimlessly. She appreciated Lizzie's pep talk, but she wasn't sure how helpful it could be. Perhaps she had hoped for too much, too quickly. Dana had never experienced that kind of loss, and she didn't even know how to talk to Holly now.

They could still be friends, couldn't they?

But that was the problem, right? She didn't want to be just friends. Only in this, it didn't matter what she wanted. She had to have patience, figure out where Holly stood—if she had simply taken her by surprise with the kiss, or if she wasn't ready at all.

Dana was afraid that she had her answer already.

Chapter Eight

HOLLY

"It's already been a long day. You can go home and finish up tomorrow." Holly looked up to find that the woman who had stepped inside the room, wasn't Claire, but Maddy Crawford, the mayor of Chestnut Hill.

"Oh, it's you."

"Yes, me. I was hoping you'd let me take you to dinner."

She and Maddy talked on a somewhat regular basis, but Holly hadn't seen her since before Dana moved to town. She wondered what kind of rumors had reached Louanne's aunt. She wanted to cry again.

"Sure, why not? I was about to leave anyway."

"You know that while I'm at it, I'll also try to convince you to come to the Christmas party. You don't have to stay long. Just be with us for a while."

"I'll think about it," Holly ascertained, prompting a smile from Maddy.

"That's more than I've gotten from you in the last years, so I'll take it."

Holly was aware of Claire's pensive gaze before they said goodbye outside the door, then Maddy drove them to *La Dolce Vita*. She couldn't help thinking how uncomplicated things had been when she'd had dinner with Dana there...She'd been incredibly naïve to think they could stay that way.

She wasn't surprised by Maddy's choice of subject either.

"So I hear that you saved a woman from bleeding to death."

Holly, however, was a bit baffled by the specific wording. Rumors could be like a game of telephone.

"If we're talking about the same woman, it wasn't quite as dramatic. Doug at the pharmacy thought she might need stitches, but we could do without. Wow. Some folks need to add some spice to every story."

"How are you doing, Holly?"

"What does that have to do with anything?" If she was acting defensive, it was because Maddy had seen right through her, and it made Holly uneasy.

"You know that Louanne loved you more than anything."

"Of course I know that." She wasn't going to cry into her lasagna. She simply wouldn't allow it.

"Then you also know she would want you to be happy."

"I am happy. I have a nice home, a satisfying job, and I...Come on, Maddy. We're not going to have that conversation."

"What conversation do you mean? You know I care about you, and so do the people in Chestnut Hill, even if some of them might go a little overboard with their good intentions. I know how hard you have grieved. We all have. But you deserve to be happy, too."

"What is all this about me being happy? I've known this woman for less than a couple of weeks! And what makes you think I'm done grieving?"

Forget about good intentions. Holly jumped to her feet and took a few bills from her wallet. "I'm sorry. I can't do this."

She fled from the table and the restaurant, snowflakes mingling with her tears.

·♥·♥·♥·♥·♥·

Holly spent the rest of the evening on her couch, trying to get warm, admitting an irrational resentment against everyone she held dear. Louanne, for leaving her alone. Everyone meaning so damn well, when they didn't understand what it was like to have all hopes and dreams ripped away abruptly. Dana, for tempting her into thinking there was something to be rebuilt from the ashes. It didn't matter that everyone thought it was the right time, giving her permission to move on. Even if she'd wanted to, she didn't know how.

She fell asleep at some point, the ringing of the phone jolting her awake. Holly was used to switching to alert right away, but the person on the other end of the line wasn't calling for her doctor skills.

"Hey. How are you?" Dana asked softly.

"Good. I think. Considering that I stormed out of a restaurant leaving a friend behind...yeah. Good. You?"

"Holly, I'm really sorry. I didn't mean to pry. Lizzie told me."

"Oh." Holly didn't know what else to say.

"I'm not good at this. I wish I was. But I wanted to know if it was okay with you that maybe, at some point, we could continue seeing each other. Not seeing each other, if that's not what you want, but...friends."

Much to her surprise, Holly felt laughter bubbling up inside of her. As if the situation wasn't already absurd enough.

"Oh God, everything would be so much easier if I knew what I wanted. For a long time, I didn't even think it was possible."

73

Dana was silent, obviously waiting for her to elaborate.

"I mean...to feel this way. About someone else. I feel like I'm cheating on her, and at the same time, I'm so afraid I could just end up in the same place, and...You don't want to hear all of this. As I pointed out to Maddy, we've only known each other for a couple of weeks. You can't be interested in this mess."

"Well, as you know I have a bit of my own mess, and you went out of your way to help me with it. I'm interested in everything. I'm interested in you."

It was Holly's turn to pause. She was fairly grateful that they didn't have this conversation face to face, after all the crying she'd done, and that was likely to come.

"There is so much I need to think about." Even as she said it, Holly was aware that thinking had little to do with it. "Would you have breakfast with me? Tomorrow...perhaps not at Marcie's this time? There's a diner near the hospital, and I think we'd have a little more privacy."

"I'd love to," Dana said without hesitation. "We're smart women, right? We can figure this out."

Again, Holly had to laugh. "I hope so. I'll see you tomorrow."

For the first time today, she felt hopeful.

·♥·♥·♥·♥·♥·

Strangely enough, she didn't cry that night, but that didn't mean her dilemma was solved in any way. Holly didn't know how to feel—she wasn't sure that there was any appropriate way. She missed Louanne every day, the life they'd had and the one they'd dreamed about, but she had also done her best to push these feelings aside after a while.

Holly didn't think anyone was ever done grieving—but the people in town still needed her, and she had stepped up. For them, and for herself so she could survive in more than one way.

It had been easier to be around Dana while she could still fool herself thinking she was helping out a stranger, or that they could even become friends.

If her feelings went beyond that, would that be acceptable—appropriate? In anyone's eyes—in her own? She had no idea.

"I could really use your help right now," she said in the silence. Of course, there was no answer. There never was.

But she fell asleep, dreaming about sitting in front of a mirror, in a wedding dress, the scene oddly serene. When Holly woke up, it was almost five o'clock. She longed to go back to that quiet, peaceful moment, but of course that wasn't possible.

She got up, showered and dressed and then went down to the practice to take care of some paperwork before she'd meet Dana.

Blessed routine. The next time she glanced at her clock, nearly two hours had passed, and it was time to go.

Dana picked her up at seven, greeting her with a hug. Holly allowed herself a moment to acknowledge that she'd deeply regret it if their story ended right here and now...She just didn't know how it could continue.

"Good morning."

"Good morning," Dana returned with a warm smile. "How are you?"

"A little embarrassed," Holly admitted. "I don't know why...I should have told you right away. I don't want to keep anything from you."

"I imagine it's hard...and just because I blurted out my whole story right away, doesn't mean you had to."

"I know. Come on, let's go eat."

They were mostly silent during the short drive. When they entered the diner, Holly realized that she had promised too much too soon. The McKenzies sat at a corner table, smiling and waving. So much for privacy.

They sat at a table by the window, the young waitress arriving a few seconds later. "Morning, ladies. What can I bring you?"

They both ordered, and when they were alone again, Holly wondered if she should explain more. If she had to.

"This took me by surprise. I mean...I have friends, and they invite me, and sometimes I go. Most of the time, once I close the practice, I just want to be by myself. I didn't even know I'd like to..." She took a deep breath. Let the chips fall where they may. "Be with someone else. It's pretty amazing. And to be honest, it's kind of freaking me out." Holly had been afraid she wouldn't be able to find words, but now it seemed she wasn't able to stop. "I, we, didn't prepare for this, not even in a joke. In case this happens, what do we do, is it okay to move on? No, that's bad. I don't want to forget, anything, but people have been telling me for a while now that I need to live my life in the present. I thought I was, but I don't know anymore."

"I don't know if that helps at all, but I don't have all the answers either. I came here to get away from it all. I'll have to find another job eventually, but I've realized I like it here. The town, the people...I've kind of fallen in love."

Holly felt a bit light-headed, eventually realizing she'd been holding her breath.

"Then again, pretty much all of it happened because of you. I guess I'm wondering if you can at all imagine...If we were taking it slow..."

"Slow is good."

"Okay. And I want you to know that I'm completely out of my depth, but if you want to talk, I'll be here, and I'll listen."

"Thank you. I think this is exactly what I need. Taking it slow, I mean. I don't know if there is so much else to talk about that the nice folks of Chestnut Hill haven't already told you..."

Dana smiled wistfully. "Yeah, I'm sorry about that. I might have pushed a little...I was worried about you."

"That's okay. They don't need to be pushed hard to engage in a little friendly meddling. I do need to go to work now, but maybe you'd like to come by tonight?"

They both knew the answer before she'd even asked the question.

Chapter Nine

DANA

B efore she went home, Dana went to the homeware store where she bought a set of dishes, utensils, and a couple of decorative pillows. It was starting to look a lot like home in the house on the hill. Now that all the windows shut tightly, and the heating worked perfectly, she had begun a thorough cleaning and was making great progress. For the future rent money...sales price...those goals had become more distant and vague than they had been before. She didn't mind.

When she arranged the pillows on the couch, her phone rang. Caller ID told her it was Annie.

"Hi."

"Hi? What's going on with you? I've called you three times already, no answer. Is everything okay?"

"Oh, yes, it's good. I'm having a good time."

"I'm glad," Annie said, sounding fairly perplexed. What, was it so hard to imagine that Dana was having a good time by herself? Of course, she wasn't alone in Chestnut Hill. Dana smiled to herself, recalling her conversation with Holly. For sure, they'd been dealt some obstacles, but that didn't mean they couldn't go anywhere from here. In fact, they would...just slow.

"I'm sorry I didn't pick up, but I was kind of busy. What's up?"

"I wanted to check if you're still up for having guests after Christmas, or did you sell the house already?"

"Of course not—I mean, sure, you're welcome."

"Are you sure everything's okay?"

"Yes! Everything's going according to plan."

"All right then. Is the twenty-seventh okay?"

"Perfect. I look forward to seeing you."

"You too. I have to go. Can't wait to see the Christmas village—it seems to have done you some good."

"Oh, it has."

The moment she ended the call, Dana felt the smile slipping from her face. It wasn't that she minded the upcoming visit. She was looking forward to seeing her friends, but the plans they'd made before her departure also reminded her of everything she hadn't tackled yet. Before she'd start the job search, she would also have to figure out what to do with the house.

Dana had done cleaning, decorating, occasional snow shoveling, and she'd bought various items to make herself more at home. She hadn't bothered to contact the real estate agency she'd used when she first bought it, or even come close to making a decision. For the first time in a long time, she'd become truly comfortable. Even if she knew it could hardly last, like this, beyond the holidays, she didn't want to get out of that state yet, especially now that she had other things to think about.

She didn't want to rush Holly, into anything, but she was also aware that the timing might be just right, for the both of them.

Wasn't it more important to take that chance rather than worry about what could be? In all their conversations, Holly had never said that there was no chance at all. She was all right with going slow, she had some things to figure out—all of that was understandable.

Dana was glad they had talked—did she have something to tell Holly as well, beyond the drama she'd shared on the first day? Perhaps, but it wasn't important in comparison. And tonight, she was going to see her again. She had better start thinking about that Christmas present.

Chapter Ten

HOLLY

When she got a moment to herself, Holly reluctantly picked up the phone and called Maddy. No matter how busy the town's mayor was, she had promised Holly that she'd always be available to her. True to her promise, she was on the line a couple of minutes later.

"Hi. I just wanted to say, thanks for not coming after me...and I'm sorry for running out on you."

"It's fine. I shouldn't have sprung things on you the way I did, but I guess I was a little too curious."

Holly chose her words as carefully as she could.

"I'm not even sure what I would have told you—or what to tell you now."

"Tell me about the nice lady everyone's talking about. I have yet to meet her."

Holly wasn't going to go into details, but there was at least one thing she knew for sure.

"We went out a few times. I like spending time with her, but I don't know if I'm ready for anything else."

"What about her? If she's serious about you, she'll give you that time."

"Come on," Holly protested, even though she and Dana had tackled that exact subject this morning. "It's only been a few days. Who knows anything within that time?"

"Well, Jack and I met, and we eloped two weeks later. Sometimes, it does work out that way. You will know what is right for you, Holly."

"Would you be mad if I didn't come to the Christmas party?"

"You haven't come in the last three years. I was never mad at you."

"Thank you, Maddy. I need to go."

Later that day, after dinner was almost ready, and she was waiting for her guest, Holly wandered around her home. She had put on some Christmas music, for the first time this year, for the first time in years.

She hadn't put away any of the pictures all over the place, memories of a time long gone, but not forgotten. She would never forget. What her life in the present would or could look like, was yet to be determined.

"I hope you're not mad at me either," she said standing in front of one of the pictures. While Holly did her best to escape, Louanne had liked to interact with the camera. Holly studied her leaning against the tree, sunlight playing in her hair. She wasn't sure how long she'd been standing in front of the framed photograph, but when the doorbell rang, she realized there were tears on her face. She had cried so much already. Christmas usually wasn't the best time, but things were changing now. Were they, really? She quickly went to wash her face and answered the door.

Dana was wearing high heeled boots and a long-sleeved black dress, her hair wound up in a messy bun. As Holly took in her appearance, reflecting that tonight, they were on a tentative date, she guiltily wished she'd put away some of the photos, if only for tonight. Not that she planned to do...anything...but she didn't want Dana to be uncomfortable either. There were so many memories in this place—perhaps she should have invited herself to the house on the hill instead.

All of a sudden, the music playing in the background seemed to mock her.

"Hi." Dana leaned in to kiss her cheek. "How was your day?"

"Nothing out of the ordinary. You?"

"Hm, let's see, while you were busy saving lives, I think I finished decorating the house. And I got this," she handed a bottle of wine in a gift bag to Holly. "How's that for a day's work?"

Despite herself, Holly had to laugh. "I'd say there's a time and place for everything? Thank you for the wine. But please, come on in, and sit." She was rambling, she realized, hoping to distract Dana from asking other questions.

Dana took in the surroundings with interest but followed Holly into the living room. A small pause ensued, bordering on awkward. Holly held up the bottle. "I'm just going to..."

"Sure."

Dana waited patiently as Holly went to get two glasses and the corkscrew, and then proceeded to open the bottle—or tried to. Why was her hand shaking all of a sudden?

"I can do it," Dana offered. Holly wasn't going to argue, and a minute later, they both sat down with a glass in hand.

"So...This is it. I'm sorry about all the pictures. I hope you don't think..." She let her words trail off.

"From what I've seen so far, it's a beautiful home. How long have you lived here?"

"We renovated it after Dr. Shepherd retired. He moved away, so we could get the whole house once I took over the practice."

"Louanne, what did she do?"

There were two ways the evening could go. They were either going to talk about Louanne, or kiss again. It couldn't be both. Holly assumed it was decided now, but with those ever-present pictures, she shouldn't have been surprised.

"She worked for the county, oversaw transportation. She liked that, actually. After I went from the hospital into my own practice, we both had better hours, and...We had planned to do so much."

"I'm sorry," Dana said softly.

"It only goes to show that you shouldn't wait to do the things you want—because you never know."

"What do you want?"

Holly leaned back into the couch, wondering if she had a real answer beyond platitudes.

"I wanted to turn back time, prevent what happened some-how...but it's impossible. Right now, I think I just want to make the best of each day. Speaking of which, you must be hungry. How about we eat?"

Somehow, she was relieved to make a bit of distance. She hadn't planned this evening, or what she wanted out of it, all too well.

Much to her surprise, she managed to relax during the course of the evening, realizing that just because they had both dressed up, it didn't mean that any more expectations were in the room. Dana had meant it when she said they'd take it slow. She had seen the pictures, she had asked careful questions, and she wasn't going to run.

They would be okay.

It seemed like minutes from the main course to coffee and dessert...and Holly knew she didn't want to offer the guest apartment again, but she also wasn't ready for anything else. She had an idea though.

"Remember that walk we wanted to take? Let's do it now."

Perhaps Dana had entertained similar questions on how to end this evening on a high note. "Sure," she said. "It's really pretty outside."

It was. Business owners and individual residents competed for the most joyful Christmas decorations. More people than usual were still outside, some coming from office parties, some simply enjoying the view. They came to the main square where the church and the town hall were located. A small Christmas market was open to residents and tourists, offering a variety of food, artwork and clothing.

"I shouldn't say that because dinner was amazing, and I couldn't eat anything else." Dana laughed softly. "But it smells amazing."

"We could come back another time for a taste."

"That would be great."

Around the Christmas tree, the city created an ice rink every year. The past few years, she had barely paid attention, the time passing in a blur. Holly admitted that for too long, she hadn't been able to stand happy people. In the context of her practice, where she helped her patients heal, supported them, it was different. Outside of that safe space, she hadn't even realized how envious and resentful she'd been to everyone who seemed to have what she had lost—not knowing that all this time, it had been up to her to go out and find...something.

"Would you like to skate?"

She had actually said it out loud, Dana's baffled expression was telling.

"Now?"

"There's no time like now. You've done it before, right?"

"A few times, but that was a while ago. I'm not sure..."

"Come on, let's try."

Dana laughed. "At least, if I break a leg, the doctor will be right there."

"Don't be silly." Holly shook her head. "You're not going to break anything. I've got you."

For some reason, this didn't feel like they were joking any longer. Dana's smile was serene rather than amused.

They did run into a problem though—the young man who rented out the skates was just about to close up the rink. Holly knew him—he was a nephew of the Petersons.

"Please, Jason, just for a few minutes. Ms. Clover is new in town, and we want to give her the best impression, right?"

"I guess so. I mean, sure." He sighed. On the bright side, the nineteen-year-old was unlikely to be interested in the Chestnut Hill rumor mill. He handed them the skates and they went to change and step onto the rink. It had been a while for Holly too, so despite her promises she was a bit unsteady at first. Eventually, Dana took her hand, and all of a sudden, the balance worked just fine. Like meant to be. Jason turned the music up slightly, playing *Rockin' Around The Christmas Tree*, *Here Comes Santa Claus*, and for an abrupt change of pace, *O Holy Night*. When was the last time she'd actually listened to any of those songs, on purpose? Truth be told, even before Louanne's tragic death, they had been busy around this time. Chestnut Hill looked idyllic to outsiders, but many of the residents couldn't, or didn't take the time to slow down for the holidays.

This felt different. And so right. When the song stopped, so did they, out of breath, reddened cheeks...Holly leaned in and kissed Dana, the heat of the kiss a pleasant contrast to the chill of their skin. There was no problem with balance any longer. A true Christmas miracle.

Jason clearing his throat startled them apart, "Um, Dr. McEwen...I really need to close up here."

"Of course. Thank you."

They walked back to Holly's front door hand in hand, the warmth between them easily withstanding the freezing temperature. So much hope. And promise. Holly was reluctant to let go as she searched for the key in her purse.

"I should go," Dana said.

Holly studied her, hoping to find an indication that they were still on the same page. Going somewhere. She wanted her to come in, throw all caution in the wind, but deep down she knew it was too early for that. Her body didn't care, but her mind was a bit more guarded.

"Let's do this again. Soon."

"Skate? Sure, it was fun."

"No, not that." In case Dana still didn't understand, Holly pulled her close for another kiss. "Good night."

Chapter Eleven

DANA

On her way back to the house, Dana turned the volume of the radio higher, Christmas full on at this station. In her mind, she replayed all the beautiful moments leading up to...Okay, that was not a good idea. She had to concentrate on driving. With the temperature slipping even more, the roads had become more slippery, and the snowplows didn't always make it to every part of her way.

Nevertheless, she made it up to the house, sighing in bliss as she stepped inside the warmth. Right now, she loved every person who had helped her get the heat back on...and one in particular. She was in love. It was real, amazing, a beautiful surprise. And why not? Maybe she'd earned it after all the unpleasant events of the past weeks. If that was the case, Holly had earned it too.

They would learn to strike a balance, between seizing the moment, and not rushing anything. It would work out, because this time, it was right, meant-to-be right.

Dana went into the bathroom and ran a hot bath. She got herself a glass of wine from the fridge that she put on the side before she stepped into the water, leaning back with a happy sigh.

She could understand why Holly needed to say goodbye at the front door. If she hadn't, they might have taken that step too early...and Dana didn't want to make a mistake, not with someone who had become this important to her. They both came with their respective history. They had to acknowledge that. But they could build a present and a future together. She had never been more certain of that.

·♥·♥·♥·♥·♥·

The ringing phone woke her the next morning.

"Annie, what time is it?"

"Ms. Clover? Can we talk?"

"Oh." She was wide awake now, sitting up in bed. This was unexpected...or perhaps she should simply stop expecting anything, because her plans never seemed to work out that way. "Mr. Marks. That's a surprise."

"I imagine."

"Is there any problem with the paperwork? According to my contract, there should be one last payment this month."

"I'm aware of that. I was wondering...if there was a way we could make you reconsider."

The seconds ticked by as Dana was trying to get a grip, understand what he'd just said, and what it could mean for her. She had claimed that she wanted to move on, from this firm, and their cases.

"What do you mean?"

"I know you're in Chestnut Hill right now. We could use your help with a client, and if everything works out...We could forget about everything that's been said."

"Just like that? I'm not sure. You still believed Mr. Cassidy over me."

He sighed. "Yes, and I wanted to apologize for that. Mr. Cassidy no longer works for the firm."

That was...news, in any case. Good or bad, for her, Dana wasn't sure.

"How do you know I'm in Chestnut Hill?"

"Ms. Clover, this is important. Our client needs someone good on this, and fast, and you'd be in the perfect position."

"It's Christmas in three days. I'm on vacation."

"I'm aware. I'll send you the file, and you get back to me first thing on the twenty-sixth?"

Dana couldn't believe what she was hearing. This was more than Marks had talked to her in her entire time with the firm.

"What's Mr. Sheldon's take on this? Senior and junior."

"They agree that these are special circumstances...and that we might have made a mistake with you and Mr. Cassidy."

Might have.

"I can look at it," she offered. That wasn't a yes or no. She'd still had options after that...There was another side to this that intrigued her. What if she could work a long-term project with a client out of Chestnut Hill? That would give her even more time to decide what to do with the house...and there was the vague prospect that she might keep it after all, not for prospective tenants, but herself.

"Thank you. That's all I'm asking."

"What client are we talking about?" She should have asked that question first—but she hadn't said yes yet, right?

"Someone who could be very good for this town. They want to make sure the paperwork is set."

"Okay then. Send me everything, and I'll get back to you."

"Thanks, Ms. Clover. We appreciate it. And Merry Christmas."

"We'll talk later. Merry Christmas, Mr. Marks."

Dana didn't waste any time. She showered, dressed and drove into town right away. It was too late to catch Holly before she opened her practice, but perhaps she could steal her for lunch later. For now, she needed some breakfast and inspiration.

This Christmas was going to be special, and not just for plans that made her smile in anticipation. She wanted to find the perfect gift for Holly.

Obviously, she was immersed in the community. Besides the glimpse into her former life, Dana had seen what she assumed to be creations of local artists in Holly's home, based on what Lizzie had told her, paintings and a couple of sculptures. She had browsed the galleries on Main Street before, and she planned to take the day to come up with something to give to Holly.

Lizzie served her breakfast, but since the café was almost three quarters filled, she was too busy to talk. Unlike the first time she'd come here alone, Dana realized that almost every other patron greeted her, on her way in and out.

Once upon a time she had lived on a corner long enough that the barista in the local coffee shop remembered her, but these things didn't happen too often in the city. Dana found that she didn't mind.

Her first stop was at a painter's gallery. Angela Rossi had captured the cozy landscapes of Chestnut Hill in all seasons. Dana stood in front of a painting that showed trees in full bloom. She hadn't even thought about staying beyond Christmas, but with the mysterious offer from Marks, maybe there was a way? Should she give up the apartment and move all the way

94

here, regardless? Would Holly ever consider moving? Probably not—and it was too early for all of this anyway.

"Hi, Ms. Clover," Angela said behind her.

"Please, it's Dana. These are beautiful."

"Thank you. It's easy to get inspired around here."

"Yes, I can see why." She turned to another painting that showed the church and town hall, with the Christmas tree and ice rink. The memory made her face warm.

"I'll come back," she promised. "Merry Christmas."

She went to a couple of more galleries without finding what she was looking for. The prices were reasonable—this was a small town. She had seen beautiful paintings and sculptures, some similar to what Holly already owned, but Dana couldn't seem to make up her mind. She'd know the perfect gift when she saw it. Hopefully, sometime before Christmas.

It was getting closer to noon. Dana debated with herself whether to go back and check in on Holly or try one more gallery first. This one was on a small side street, and a few steps were leading down to what looked like a basement apartment with a big window.

Okay. One more.

She went down the winding stairs into a store that felt near claustrophobic. There was a bit of everything: Paintings, sculptures, decorative articles, and a bit of jewelry. She saw a few pairs of nice earrings, pausing, before her gaze fell on the necklace. It was made of silver-framed pieces, shimmering in different shades of blue. It looked absolutely stunning.

Dana looked around, but she couldn't see anyone. There wasn't any sort of bell either. What person left a place with precious items like these all alone? Not that she was going to steal any of it, but she would have liked to see Holly today.

"Hello?"

Finally, a backdoor almost hidden in the wall opened, and a tall, dark-haired woman stepped outside. "Oh, hi. I'm so sorry, but there was something I needed to take care of back there...You found something you like?"

"Yes, I'd like this one. Could you gift-wrap it, please?"

"Of course. Christmas always comes so fast, doesn't it?" the woman chatted before she put the necklace in a gift box, and wrapped it with a red bow. "Someone special, huh?"

"Absolutely. Thank you."

She hurried back to Marcie's Café where she bought three coffees and sandwiches to go.

Claire's eyes widened when she saw Dana's offerings.

"You thought of me? That is so nice of you. I was starving...well, I know you shouldn't say that, but this looks amazing. Thank you so much."

Dana couldn't help but laugh at her enthusiastic response.

"It's no problem. Besides, it wouldn't be nice to have lunch with Holly and not bring you any."

Claire took a sip of the coffee, her expression pure bliss.

"Hm, I'm afraid she can't take a break right now." She nodded to the almost filled waiting room. "I can give it to her when she has a minute..."

"That's okay, thank you. Could you tell her I'll call her tonight?"

Dana realized that a few of the town's residents waiting to see Holly wore the same knowing smile Claire did. She was strangely fine with it.

Chapter Twelve

HOLLY.

Only three days until Christmas. This time, it had really caught her by surprise. In the past years, Holly had taken measures to cut herself off from the cheeriness best she could, but she had neglected all of those measures. Instead, she'd gone on dinner dates, taken walks, gone skating...She wasn't ready yet to go to Maddy's Christmas party. Holly wanted to spend as much time as possible with Dana, and bringing another woman to the Crawfords' Christmas party would be strange, for everyone involved.

She knew that Dana's friends planned to visit after Christmas, but there was still time—important time they could spend together, important steps to take. When she was back in her apartment after the workday, she left her cell phone on the counter in the bathroom when she took a shower, anxious that she might miss the call. It came when she had just put on a fluffy robe.

"Busy day, huh?"

"Yes, but the sandwich was great, thank you for that. You made Claire very happy, too."

"To be honest, she was not my priority," Dana admitted. "Okay, I'm sorry, that sounds bad. I knew you were both busy."

"We appreciated it." All of a sudden, the distance seemed too much. Holly had no idea how to express that feeling, though. She hesitated to put something in words she wouldn't be able to take back.

"Have you had dinner yet?" Dana focused on more pragmatic things. Holly was sick and tired of pragmatic.

"I'm not wearing many clothes right now..."

"Oh. That's something nice to imagine."

"No, what I mean is...I could get dressed again, and come by? To answer your question, no, I haven't had anything since lunch, and I don't feel like eating alone...or at Marcie's, where everyone is going to ask me where you are. Actually...I want to be where you are. Would you be okay with that?"

To her relief, Dana's answer was quick and unambiguous. "Absolutely. I can't wait."

After ending the call, Holly made a quick trip to the master bedroom and bathroom, putting a few items into her bag. She was almost out of the door, but stepped back, in front of that same picture.

"Thank you," she whispered, and left.

As she drove past houses and yards illuminated by Christmas lights, there wasn't a doubt in her mind. For once, even the fear of the next bad thing to happen was distant. She didn't regret taking her time to live her grief, her worries and her reservations. She'd needed to come to those conclusions by herself, and there was no shortcut well meaning neighbors could create.

After parking her car in the usual spot, she nearly ran up the stairs to the front door.

"I'm glad you had time tonight," Dana said as she opened the door. "I didn't expect that, but I went grocery shopping yesterday, and I—"

Holly cut her off with a kiss that left no doubts as to her motivation, and to her relief, Dana didn't seem to have any questions either.

"On the other hand, food can wait." Then she had a couple of questions after all. "Don't you want to take off your coat?" And "Are you sure?"

Holly realized that she was serious, and if she had wanted to turn around, or spend the evening watching TV, Dana would have gone along with it. That only made her more certain. "I haven't been so sure of anything in a long time," she said.

·♥·♥·♥·♥·♥·

It was still true when she stood in Dana's bedroom, shivering with pleasure as Dana pulled down the zipper of her dress, kissing the exposed skin. She had to smile at the thought that everything started with a broken heating system. It was definitely hot in the room at this moment.

"What's funny?" Dana asked, running her fingertips up and down Holly's arms.

Her dress fell to the floor, and she turned in Dana's embrace.

"Just thinking how nice and warm it is in here...I'm so glad you got that worked out."

"Me too."

Holly leaned into her, feeling Dana gasp when she placed her lips against her neck. She had lived without this kind of intimacy long enough to fool herself into thinking she could probably do without altogether. Every second, every touch, proved her wrong. She was hungry for so much more. Fortunately, she had found a lover who was happy to give her everything she desired. She might feel differently tomorrow morning, but for the moment, her life was nothing short of magic.

Chapter Thirteen

DANA

They had been resting for a few minutes, but she was still breathless. Holly was warm and relaxed in her arms, on the verge of falling asleep. If they did that, they'd never have dinner and wake up hungry in the middle of the night, but she wasn't tempted to get up, too comfortable in the present moment. She couldn't stop touching her, running her hand down her back, reveling in the feel of smooth skin. Taking it slow.

"Maybe I don't rent out the house after all." That was not taking it slow, but perhaps she didn't care anymore. All her life she had planned everything to the last detail, and it hadn't worked out so well for her. Maybe this was better, the way it should be.

Holly raised her head, her expression between hopeful and alarmed.

"What does that mean?"

"I kind of like living here. I had no idea how much I would like it."

"Well, I don't know how many people file lawsuits around here, but I would love it if you stayed."

Dana almost told her that she might have an assignment that would allow her to do so, at least for the foreseeable future. She didn't. There would be time for that as soon as she had figured out what it was Marks wanted her to do. Even he had agreed to give her Christmas.

She kissed Holly softly in answer. "We'll see. If I get rid of the apartment...I'll have to go back anyway to wrap some things up. You could come with me...maybe take a week? But right now, I think we should eat."

"What was for dinner anyway?" Holly asked, making both of them crack up with laughter. Food had been the last thing on their minds from the moment she arrived.

"Would you be okay with some soup and a grilled cheese sandwich? I still have some wine from the other time."

"Sounds perfect."

As they both put on clothes, Dana wondered if they could do this, skip a step, be together without another deep, difficult conversation.

"Don't worry," Holly said as if reading her thoughts. "I want to be here. I didn't have to think about it long and hard...I did think about it though, and I'm all good if you are."

In the kitchen, Dana put a pot and a pan on the stove.

"I know this isn't easy for you."

"You make it pretty easy for me."

Dana gave her a quick smile before she started preparing dinner.

"That's what I hoped...Would you mind getting the wine out of the fridge?"

"Coming right up." Holly took out the bottle, found two glasses in the cabinet and poured one for each of them.

The cooking, if not especially elaborate, helped her relax. Looking at Holly who stood leaning against the counter comfortably, sipping her wine, made Dana realize that perhaps they had successfully circumvented those complications, if not as slowly as they'd imagined. And why wait if they could have something so amazing now? She had waited for many things that never arrived, thinking patience would pay off. She would have managed to be more patient if Holly had asked her to, but that didn't seem to be necessary.

"I can't tell you how glad I am you came here," she said. Nothing could be closer to the truth.

Holly leaned close for another kiss, and Dana almost burned the bread.

·♥·♥·♥·♥·♥·

They set the table in the living room and sat down to eat.

"So, have you made any plans for Christmas?" She hoped the fact that Holly was here, three days before the day, meant that she hadn't. Dana could imagine ways to spend the day...and the night before.

"Maddy asked me to come to her Christmas party. I haven't gone in years, but I think I might get a different invitation this time...?"

"Absolutely. If you don't mind that it's going to be just the two of us..."

"That's perfect. I'll open the practice for a few hours on Christmas Eve, but after that I can be all yours."

"I love the sound of that. And I promise I'll plan the meal better than this one."

"This is great."

"Sure?"

"Yes."

It would all work out now, Dana was sure. Her friends who had seen her fairly devastated on the day her world came tumbling down, would be so happy for her. She'd work with a local client, and maybe be able to start building a clientele. She could rent something in town for an office.

She had struggled at first, when her routine had been so rudely interrupted, only to find that what she had needed was a way out of said routine, find a new home. With Holly.

"It's decided then. For Christmas, you're all mine."

"It would appear so."

Chapter Fourteen

HOLLY

D ana had made a fire in the fireplace. The flames were almost hypnotic, their warmth making her sleepy. They had almost finished the wine, and the radio played *Winter Wonderland*. She wasn't going anywhere.

A part of her was still slightly confused, wondering how the past and present could truly be merged, if they had to be, or if she could just step into the new, unknown. All she knew was that at the moment, she felt safe, something that had eluded her for years. The certainty that everything and anyone you loved could be taken away all of a sudden had changed her. And yet, here she was, trusting again. Despite their respective reassurances, this was faster than she had imagined, and to her surprise, that didn't bother her. It felt right. That was all she could acknowledge at the moment. She knew that Louanne had truly loved her, so perhaps she would want her to be happy even now, like this.

"You know, when you lose somebody, it really messes with your mind."

Oops. She hadn't meant to say that, but the alcohol had loosened her tongue. For someone who advised people how not to overdo it during the holidays, and in general, she had fallen short a little. But she had Dana's attention, and she had to make sense of what she'd said for both of them. "I mean, you can't really be angry at them, right? They didn't choose this. But you are, so angry, because they leave you behind, and the life you had, it's just gone. Then you feel bad for feeling guilty, on top of missing them so much you think you're going to die too. It's not like that anymore—but I still miss her."

"I can imagine."

"I realize I have to let go of some expectations, but it doesn't mean this can't be something good. Something we've both hoped for." She sat up and pulled up her feet under her. "Also, we don't have to talk about me all the time."

"I know, but things were a bit easier for me. My girlfriend didn't die. She just stopped loving me, though perhaps she never did. Well, I prefer not to think about it too much. I sure made mistakes, and we stopped talking. So...be ready for a lot of talking."

Holly laughed. "I'm fine with that."

Chapter Fifteen

DANA

They shared an early breakfast before Holly left for work, and when Dana checked her emails shortly after, she realized Marks had sent her the information on the case he wanted her to look into. The clients' needs were pretty cut and dried: They wanted to buy property in Chestnut Hill to build a hotel, but rather than making it a modern complex, they intended to go with existing structures. That approach intrigued her—she had yet to learn more about the history of the town, but it seemed that many of the buildings were quite old.

She looked up the address, and realized it was the block that held the building where she'd found Holly's gift. Coincidence? Fate? She still wanted to enjoy Christmas, but the more she read about the project, the more it made sense to her. Chestnut Hill depended a great deal on tourism. Finding accommodations in authentic surroundings would certainly support the industry. It would be her job to oversee the legal aspects of the transactions, and the changes that could be made to the buildings while still respecting their heritage.

So far, so good, right? This could be extremely helpful, to get her back into the good graces of Sheldon & Marks for a while, with a client she didn't despise, and the prospect of making a name for herself in Chestnut Hill—which would mean that she might be able to practice here. Stay. Make a home. The idea had sounded good with the first coffee, by the third she was determined. They could both have their own businesses and remind each other to make time for other things as well.

Dana picked up the phone and called Marks who, miraculously, was in his office and took her call right away.

"I didn't expect to hear from you so soon," he said.

"I can start after Christmas like we agreed. I'd like to do this, actually. I think businesses in Chestnut Hill would benefit, and so would our clients, of course."

"Good. Get in touch with the client and have them come over as soon as possible. Glad to have you back, Ms. Clover."

"Thanks," she said. "This is a good project. I'm glad to be on board."

He didn't offer her anything beyond that. Dana hadn't expected it either. She was going to look into rental space in town. While you couldn't predict everything, it couldn't hurt to be prepared.

·♥·♥·♥·♥·♥·

Putting work aside for a while, Dana joined Holly for the Christmas Eve service after Holly had closed her practice until the 26th. Even after the time she'd spent here, Dana was surprised how much she enjoyed the community coming together, celebrating. It made her even happier to think that she was almost part of that community, and that she would be able to do something to help it thrive even more.

In the choir, she recognized Lizzie, the woman who had sold her the necklace, and a few other people she'd briefly met on her quest to make the house on the hill more of a home. Their rendition of traditional carols was beautiful and haunting. It was as if for the first time since childhood, she understood what Christmas truly meant. She didn't care anymore if she was getting ahead of herself—both she and Holly understood that waiting too long might be worse than going too fast. She was happy to share those days with someone she was falling in love with. Someone who had rescued her quite literally.

From blood poisoning and loneliness. Dana couldn't keep the smile off her face.

"What's on your mind?" Holly whispered.

"You are."

After the service ended, they headed back to the house on the hill, heart and minds warmed with the spirit of the season, and sweet anticipation.

·♥·♥·♥·♥·♥·

This time of year usually passed in a blur, especially since she hadn't had the chance to take this much time off in years. New snow, Christmas carols and an amazing encounter seemed to have slowed down everything, and Dana didn't mind a bit. She was full of hope for what the New Year would bring—and whatever happened, she wanted Holly in it.

She couldn't bring herself to wait until the next morning, so around midnight, she slipped out of bed and got the wrapped present out of the cabinet where she'd put it for the time being. She woke Holly who went from deep sleep to one hundred percent alert within seconds.

"What happened? Are you okay?"

"Everything is fine. I wanted to give you this."

"Right now?" Holly sat up against the headboard, amused. "You couldn't wait until tomorrow morning?"

"I didn't want to. Wow...I hope I'm not way overselling this, but I thought it was really beautiful...You're beautiful." Holly's soft smile made her relax and take a deep breath. The moment the necklace was revealed, Dana knew she had made the perfect choice. Holly looked up at her in wonder and surprise.

"How could you know? This is...I don't know what to say. Thank you so much." She leaned forward to kiss Dana, and then embrace her tightly. "I love it. I absolutely love this place, and the last time I went, I saw this. Needless to say, I didn't get it. I was thinking, why bother—I won't wear it in the practice, and I don't go anywhere."

"But that's not true anymore."

"No, it isn't. I imagine I should get you your gift."

She pushed back the covers and got out of bed, walking over to the suitcase she'd brought. Dana realized that the package she produced was quite a bit bigger than the one that had held the necklace. Something soft was inside, and she quickly tore the thin paper away. Her hands touched soft, warm fabric, a thick blanket in warm tones.

"Yours is so much nicer," Holly said, sounding a tad nervous, "but I thought about how we met, and how you injured yourself trying to get warm."

"Yeah. That was stupid."

"No. No! That's not what I meant. I wanted to give you something to keep you warm. Especially now that you said you might want to stay in town, which would be amazing...but it gets chilly a lot up here, even in the spring."

"It's great. Thank you so much." She was touched by the thoughtful gift, and hoped she hadn't gotten ahead of herself, buying jewelry—but Holly loved local artistry, and this was a part of it. Dana thought they'd both done well, trying to give something meaningful to someone who had quickly come to mean a lot to them. "Not only did you keep me warm—and continue to do so—but you also saved me from suffering a tetanus infection. How can I thank you?"

"Just be here," Holly whispered, and it was the easiest thing Dana had ever done.

Chapter Sixteen

HOLLY

H olly was living in a dream. At least, it was hard to believe that this could be her reality, after the doubts, the
despair, and the harrowing grief. She was so grateful that Dana
understood the pace at which she needed to take each step, even
if it meant her gift might have been more appropriate for a
friend than a lover. She was happy to live in a place where her
friends and neighbors all contributed to creating a safe, loving
environment. Each of their kindness and talents meant a lot
to her, and now she could share all of this with Dana. It was
Christmas Day—barely—and she wasn't alone, trying to drown
herself in work. She felt serene, safe—in love, even. She wanted
to stay in this place forever.

They woke up to a chilly, but beautiful sunny Christmas
morning. Together, they cooked an elaborate breakfast, with
French toast, bacon, poached eggs. Was it possible that even
food tasted different? She had enjoyed Marcie's cuisine once a

week, and for the rest of the time, eaten because she had to, but every sensation seemed more intense.

Dana had said that Holly saved her, but she wondered if it was really the other way around.

"I think I should invest in a dishwasher," Dana said as they were starting to clear away the dishes. "No matter what I decide, it could be practical."

"Sure."

Holly was momentarily distracted by the sight of a car coming up the hill, and parking in front of the house. She saw three women exit it, all of them unfamiliar. Dana's friends weren't going to come by until later? She wasn't ready, she realized. Wanting Dana to herself for a little longer was only a part of it, but a big part.

Nevertheless, the doorbell rang.

"This is strange," Dana said. "I hope no one's trying to reach you. I was hoping you could stay a bit longer."

"Me too. But I don't think..."

She had already gone to open the door. Holly watched Dana's expression turn from pleasantly surprised to openly irritated.

"What's going on?" Dana asked, her tone a bit too sharp to greet good friends. The ones who had announced their visit, were a couple, Annie and Kristen, Holly remembered. Who was the third woman? The answer came to her all of a sudden, even before Tricia moved and wrapped Dana in a close hug.

"I missed you so much!" she exclaimed.

Holly stood, the dishtowel in hand, frozen. She wanted to disappear, but of course the guests, all of them, had noticed her by now.

Dana quickly stepped out of her ex's embrace.

"Look, I have no idea what you're all doing here, today, but I guess someone is going to explain things to me? Annie?"

"I'm sorry, I didn't know…" Annie cast an apologetic look at Holly. "Anyway, we thought we'd surprise you, and someone had the idea to tag along last minute."

"I see," Dana said, coolly. "Tricia, I'm sorry, too. I didn't invite you."

"No…but we need to talk."

"No, we don't. Everything that needed to be said, we said the last time. I've moved on."

Holly couldn't help cringing. Of course, Tricia had brought this on herself by sleeping with another woman, but still. She realized with dread that she might be the one to have overstayed her welcome soon, in case Dana changed her mind. Would she? And even if she didn't, it was Christmas. She couldn't ask Dana to send her friends back home.

"It's Christmas," Annie said. "Can't we all sit down for a moment?"

Holly waited a few seconds, maybe hoping that Dana would say something definitive that would end this bizarre situation, and they'd be able to get back to their perfect, dreamy holiday. She cleared her throat, all eyes on her in an instant.

"I think you all have some things to talk about," she said. "I need to get to the practice, so…I'll see you."

"Wait." Dana sounded impatient, though Holly wasn't sure if it was directed at her, or at the general situation. "Your car isn't here."

"I was hoping I could take yours? You could get it when you come into town, or I'll bring it later…" Being the subject of all those curious gazes made her fidgety and flustered. With a sigh, Dana went to get her keys, following her upstairs.

"You don't have to explain," Holly said as she put her clothes in her suitcase.

"There's nothing to explain. I'll send Tricia home. Hell, I'll even pay for a rental car. I don't want her here."

"Good luck finding that rental." Holly found that her lame attempt at a joke made her want to cry.

"I can't believe she's about to ruin our Christmas too." Dana looked alarmed all of a sudden. "But we're okay, right? You don't think I had anything to do with this?"

"Of course not." Holly couldn't even begin to convey all the complicated emotions she had, being reminded of that other life Dana had, back in New York, with friends, and an ex who obviously still had high hopes. Could she really fit into that, any way? All she knew was that for the moment, she needed time to think. Dana handed her the keys, her gaze full of regret.

"I'll clear this up for good, I promise. Come back soon. And I don't mean that I need the car. I need you."

Holly was grateful for the reassurance. She wasn't sure it was enough, but she had to go with it for now. She, too, had another life outside these four walls.

Chapter Seventeen

DANA

After Holly had left, Dana stood on the porch, cranky and unwilling to face her meddling friends just yet. What were they thinking? They had seen how devastated she was after finding out Tricia had cheated—and perhaps she had overreacted, should have seen it coming. She didn't think she had given any of them any indication that she was open to getting back together, least of all Tricia.

Then why was she feeling a tad guilty? There was no reason. Sure, she had become involved with Holly rather quickly, but that was no one's business but Holly's and hers. Shivering, and even crankier for it, she turned and went back inside the house.

Her guests were sitting in the living room, literally on the edge of their seats, their postures tense.

Dana shook her head. "Annie, let's have a word in private."

Tricia got to her feet. "Dana, please, can't we talk—"

"No," Dana said, holding up her hand. She spun around and walked into the kitchen, Annie following her hesitantly. When they were out of the others' earshot, she began, "Are you out of your mind?"

"I see the timing was bad. I'm sorry. Would you by any chance have some coffee left?"

"Focus! What the hell is Tricia doing here? I seem to remember you told me I could do so much better than a girlfriend who cheats on me. I took your advice to heart, and now you want me to take her back? This is ridiculous. I'm really disappointed."

"I said I was sorry," Annie defended herself. "I meant it at the time, but Tricia came to see us, and she feels horrible about what she did."

"As she should."

"Yes, but we had no idea what was going on here." Annie sighed. "We thought you two could work it out, especially since...it's Christmas."

"Oh, give me a break, Christmas has nothing to do with it. And there's nothing to work out. Tricia felt neglected, she was unhappy, I get that. She could have talked to me, suggested we take a break, break up, whatever. Instead, she was sleeping with someone else behind my back."

"Yes, and I know that makes me a bad person. I will regret that for the rest of my life," Tricia, who had walked in silently, said. She had tears in her eyes. Perhaps it was the influence of this town, everything she had found here—and okay, maybe a little, Christmas—Dana found her anger was dissipating.

"There's no point in that. I forgive you. I just don't want us to be in a relationship."

"One mistake, and you throw me away?"

"How many times did you repeat that mistake?"

Tricia blushed.

"Okay, here goes nothing," Annie summed up the conversation. "Tricia, I'm sorry, I warned you that this could go either way."

"Well, thanks for pointing that out now," Tricia snapped and rushed out of the room.

Dana leaned against the counter and reached up to massage her forehead. Hard to believe that only a few hours ago, she and Holly were cuddling in bed, daydreaming about the fabulous, lazy time they were going to have until it was back to work for both of them.

"Do you want us to leave?" Annie asked softly. "I mean...there's probably some place we could stay."

"I want her to leave, but since she came with you, I'm not sure how to handle that. I think I need some coffee too."

As she prepared a new batch, Dana thought that she didn't need to ruin the vacation for her well-meaning, but misguided friends. This was a temporary challenge—and maybe Holly could help her out one more time. She planned on making it up to her, no matter what, or how long, it took.

The phone jolted her out of her thoughts. Dana pushed the button on the coffeemaker, picking up as the coffee was starting to brew.

Chapter Eighteen

HOLLY

Holly wasn't going to her practice. Instead, she drove straight to the Crawford estate. She was too restless and worried to be alone right now—worried that she might have made a huge mistake, that she should have stepped back while she still could.

And how naïve and easy had she been, going out with Dana a few hours after they'd met? Easy. Needy. She was crying already.

When the door opened, Holly was immediately hit by the smell of food. It was possible that for a moment, she had forgotten that it was Christmas Day, and most people, including the Crawfords, were busy celebrating. However, Maddy's expression was serious.

"Come on in, Holly. We have to talk."

For a moment, Holly was confused. How could she know? Had Annie, Kristen and Tricia stopped somewhere on the way, had somebody overheard something...? No. Chestnut Hill's grapevine wasn't that fast. Chances were Maddy had something entirely different on her mind.

"Okay. Sure."

"Please, I'd love you to stay for lunch after. Let's go to my office first."

At this point, Holly was alarmed. "What is wrong?" she asked.

Maddy waited until they sat in her office. She had closed the door.

"My apologies, if this is a little personal—I'll explain in a moment. You and Ms. Clover, how serious is it?"

Holly had trouble reacting appropriately, when her jaw was dropping, and her eyes were welling up at the same moment.

"You're right, it's personal, but...I wish I knew. I think...I'm in love with her, and it scares the hell out of me. Her ex wants to get back together."

"Oh. And she wants that too?"

"No. I don't think so. I'm sorry I'm bothering you with this. It's just...what did you want to talk about?"

"You're not bothering me. I asked. Holly, there's something else you should know."

All of a sudden, her worries seemed small and insignificant. Maddy had the lives of everyone in Chestnut Hill to consider.

"What's going on?"

"I've been approached by several business owners today. There's someone going around, one of those big corporations, making them offers."

"What kind of offers?" Fairly relieved about the distraction, Holly was no less confused.

"They want to buy a whole block to build a new hotel complex. I have to look further into that, but from what I hear, they are pretty persuasive. Could it be a good thing for Chestnut

Hill, maybe, but I'm not sure that once they have their hands on the real estate, they'll have all our best interests in mind."

Holly agreed. "We don't really need that here, do we? We have enough places for tourists to stay, in and around Chestnut Hill...and in the old town, one of those complexes would stand out like a sore thumb. That's where they want to build it, right?"

"That's right. And they're represented by a law firm called Sheldon & Marks. Ms. Clover's employer."

"No. You must be mistaken. The whole reason why Dana came here is...they were about to fire her for some mistake someone else made, but she quit first. She's not with them anymore."

Maddy looked doubtful. "Well, that's not what I heard. Folks are worried. Most of them don't want to sell, but some might have to, and I'm not sure what that's going to do to the profile of our town. They expect me to protect them, but of course I need more information. Do you think you could talk to her about this?"

"I don't know. I could...Dana didn't mention any of this to me, so, maybe..."

She didn't want Holly to know? She reflected back on the time they'd spent together, talking, laughing, falling in love...Holly couldn't imagine that Dana's sole reason for coming to Chestnut Hill had been to seal the deal, but now this was on her mind, and she had trouble getting rid of the thought.

"I don't claim to know what her motives are," Maddy said. "But I think we'd all feel better if we found out."

Holly wasn't so sure. She'd stay for the meal and try to gather her thoughts before confronting Dana. She didn't have much of an appetite. Was it too much to ask to return to those beautiful moments, just hours ago? What if they'd never been anything but an illusion?

Chapter Nineteen

DANA

When Dana realized who the caller was, she asked Annie to serve the coffee, and went into the bedroom. Absentmindedly, she ran her hand over the soft blanket Holly had given her—last night instead of this morning, because Dana had woken her in the middle of the night.

"Today? It's Christmas."

"I'm aware," Marks said. "I thought you said you could do this."

"Yes, sure, I can meet with the clients today if it's that urgent."

It might not be such a bad thing to give Holly some space and leave her friends and Tricia to their own devices. She could prove to Holly that she had moved on, that she was trying to lay a foundation for her life here. For sure she wasn't going to work for Sheldon & Marks forever. There had to be a way she could make a living here in Chestnut Hill.

"Great. Thank you, Ms. Clover," Marks said. "They want to move fast, have the structure up by next season."

"Yeah, about that. I imagine that will be a subject of the meeting, but I looked into some of those plans. They won't be able to build from scratch even if all the shop owners sell. Some of those buildings are under protection."

"Were, Ms. Clover. I trust that you'll be able to work a little magic, and besides, I talked to a friend of mine. Those silly regulations will soon be gone, and that will make room for innovation. Aren't you glad to be a part of it?"

Dana didn't answer right away. She had seen what the kind of "innovation" he was talking about looked like. Corporations like their clients routinely bought vast amounts of real estate and tore down centuries-old buildings. The goal was to replace them with skyscrapers that all looked the same, offering over-priced housing.

Her perfect Christmas was about to turn into a nightmare.

"I'm all for progress," she said. "We will have to honor the existing contracts though."

"Look, Dana." He sounded much too patient for her liking. "This hotel will be built either way. I thought I was giving you a chance here. You want it or not?"

"I'll get back to you after the meeting," Dana said and ended the call. She had some more research to do before meeting the client.

·▾·♥·♥·▾·♥·

A little over two hours later, Dana was glad she had done exactly that. She couldn't believe the extent to which the client, a real estate corporation with offices all over the world, and Marks, had tried to misrepresent their intentions.

The meeting took place in the conference of a hotel room outside of Chestnut Hill, and less than fifteen minutes into it, she already had enough.

"Explain this to me, please," she said. "When this project was first introduced to me, the idea was to turn existing structures into a hotel complex. What you're talking about now is something completely different, and from what I've learned, near impossible."

At this point, Dana was sure she wouldn't be able to see this through for the client. The current strategy suggested to blatantly lie to current owners, and, from what she'd been able to determine, they'd be ripped off in the process.

"Oh, don't worry, Ms. Clover, nothing is impossible," the low-level executive they'd send to represent the company, assured her. Small fish, she realized, nothing they'd send the CEO for. "Our concept is modern and sustainable, and that's what the people in this town will want."

"What's not sustainable about working with the structures of the protected buildings? Trying to get those protections revoked will cost a lot of time and money."

"Didn't Mr. Marks update you? He should have. We have connections to a congressman who can help with that. Within the next few days, we should get the go-ahead, and most of those shops are willing to sell anyway. Which is not a surprise—they'll never see that kind of money selling a few scarves and paintings."

"And you told them that you're planning to tear it all down?"

He shrugged. "Why would they care? They can always start over somewhere else if they want to. We will attract tourists who come with money to spend. Everybody wins."

Dana wasn't so sure of that. "Well, I assume the congressman is celebrating Christmas with his family today."

"Sure, but he's on it. As soon as the snow melts, we'll get the bulldozers in here, and we'll be able to rent out once fishing season starts. That's a thing around here too, I've been told. This town will see its biggest Christmas season next year—I'll be damned if that's not a miracle."

"So, what do you need me for?" Dana asked, making a weak effort to hide her frustration.

"Mr. Marks told us you've been here for a while. You know some of the people here, and we think you could help us sell the idea. Soften them up a bit, if you will."

Dana understood exactly what he meant, and it wasn't a pretty picture. On the bright side, there might be something she could do to avoid the worst-case scenario for Chestnut Hill.

"I'll have to talk to a few people," she said. "In the meantime, keep me up to date regarding those building permits."

"Mr. Marks assured us you're right for the job. I hope he was right."

"I will do everything possible for a good outcome," Dana said, and they shook hands.

She had taken Annie's car, because Holly had left with hers. After the meeting, she didn't want to go back to the house on the hill just yet—she didn't feel like being a gracious host. It was most important that she'd talk to Holly, for many reasons. Dana wanted to apologize, but at the moment, the fate of Chestnut Hill took priority.

She found her own car parked in front of Holly's building. Pausing briefly, she wondered if she should have brought a peace offering, but Marcie's Café and all the shops on Main Street were closed today. Everyone was having a peaceful time with their families. With a sigh, Dana rang the doorbell. A few seconds later, Holly buzzed her in, and she went inside, bypassing the practice to climb the stairs to the apartment.

Holly stood in the doorway, her expression unreadable.

"We need to talk."

"You don't owe me any apology where your girlfriend is concerned." However, Holly stepped aside to let her in.

"Ex-girlfriend, you know that. I wanted to apologize anyway. I could have handled it better, but..." Dana shook her head. "I didn't know what to do, or where to send them. Actually, they're still in the house, so I was wondering if I could stay with you."

"I don't think that's a good idea."

"Wait, what? I mean, why? You don't think I want to get back together with her? I don't! I caught her in bed with another woman! That's a deal breaker for me."

"I get that. I really do. But there's something else that bothers me. Why didn't you tell me that your firm sent you for the big real estate deal?"

How was it possible that Holly already knew about this? After an uncomfortable pause, Dana spoke.

"You know that's not true. I told you what happened. They contacted me a few days ago, and I thought I—" Perhaps she'd look utterly ridiculous trying to explain how this was supposed to be a stepping stone to her new life in Chestnut Hill. "The thing is that time is running out on us. They want to buy those buildings as soon as possible, and they want to tear down the whole block."

"Why are you telling me this, when you are working with them?"

"I am not...I want to help."

"How? Apparently they're going to wield all that power to drive people out of their businesses. They're a multi-million-dollar corporation, why do you think they'll listen to anything you say?"

"Holly, why are you so angry with me? I didn't know what they were planning. Converting some of the space into a hotel, yes, but I only learned today that they want to build from scratch."

"Maybe it's because I'm not so sure anymore about anything you said! What am I supposed to believe? You claimed that you were done with the job, and Tricia, and yet both are somehow involved in this. I don't know. It's all a bit too much to be a coincidence."

"But that's what it is!"

"I'm sorry. I can't deal with this right now. Perhaps we did go a little too fast...I need some time, okay? Maybe it's for the better. These things would have come up at some point anyway, right?"

"Holly. Who can I talk to around here to help sort out this mess? I swear I didn't know."

"I'm not saying all of this is your fault," Holly said, sounding tired. "Nor do I expect you to solve everything. I just need some time to myself."

"Can I call you?"

"Please, sort out what you need to sort out. I'll do the same, and we'll see what happens after that."

"All right then." Dana was halfway to the door when she turned around. "There has to be something we can do! They told me that a friend of theirs would try to scrap some of the regulations that protect those buildings, but I doubt it's that easy."

"Money makes it that easy. Don't worry. It's not really your problem, is it? It's not your home."

Those words convinced Dana that she had no good reason to stay.

·♥·♥·♥·♥·♥·

She finally drove back to the house, resigned to the fact that Annie, Kristen and Tricia were going to stay overnight—and she had nowhere else to go. At least she had filled fridge and pantry, expecting to spend a few days in with Holly before her friends arrived.

She found that the three of them apparently hadn't moved. The coffee cups were still on the table.

"Okay, you can stay here for one night. There are a couple of guest rooms, suit yourself. I'm going to make dinner."

Chastised, they got up to take the dishes into the kitchen and put away their luggage. Instead of getting started on dinner, Dana sank into the sofa, resting her head in her hands. This was supposed to be Christmas, not Groundhog Day. Everything that had gone wrong, was going wrong all over again.

Annie came back to join her a few minutes later.

"Seems to me like there's a lot I don't know," she said wistfully.

"That's not an exaggeration."

"How did the meeting go?"

"Perfect, I think, from the clients' point of view. They want me to convince shop owners to sell at a ridiculous price, so they can tear down centuries-old buildings and put a luxury resort in their place—and now Holly is convinced that I'm somehow working with them."

"Aren't you?"

"Yes...no...I don't want to do this. I want to help the people here, but I'm not sure where to start. That corporation already has a congressman in their pocket."

"Who?" Annie asked.

"Does it matter? They just wanted me to put a friendly face on the proposals. They're determined to get it done any way, with or without me."

"Well, Tricia told me on the way here that one of her friends works for a congressman, not far from here. What are the odds that he could be the same guy?"

"Tricia. Great."

Annie laid a hand on her shoulder. "I know what we need to do. Dinner. And wine. After that, we'll talk about the next steps. How does that sound?"

Dana didn't say what was really on her mind—that she didn't have any better offer at the moment. She couldn't forget what Holly had said to her.

When Tricia returned to the living room, Annie said, "Dana needs a favor."

"Of course." Tricia's face lit up. She looked happy to be given the chance. "Tell me what vegetables to chop, I'll do it."

"Tricia. A different kind of favor."

"You owe me," Dana added.

"I'm aware. What do you need?"

This had to work out. She wanted Chestnut Hill to be her home. Dana realized she'd have to fight harder for it than she had imagined.

Chapter Twenty

HOLLY

She sat alone over a frozen dinner, with a glass of wine. Holly had already bandaged the hand of a patient whose knife had slipped while he was carving turkey, written prescriptions for a couple of residents stricken with a bad case of strep throat and talked to a young woman who had just gone through a break-up and hated everything Christmas.

Not that Holly could blame her—she had fallen for the same exaggerated expectations that plagued many of her patients. Everything was supposed to be perfect, and break-ups and arguments didn't have a place in that vision.

She wondered if she'd been too harsh on Dana. Was it possible that the law firm's clients had kept her in the dark initially?

Would Tricia spend the night?

She started crying. Time went by, and Holly couldn't seem to figure out what was triggering it, or how to stop. Food and wine certainly didn't help. She had put the dishes in the sink, and opened another bottle of wine, before it came to her...The ridiculous, unnecessary argument, over...what, exactly? It had faded in her memory, but the question came back to plague her. She and Louanne had their disagreements, sometimes passionately, but they always made up, never went to bed angry...except for that one time. Holly had gone to work early in the morning, and the next time she saw Louanne, it was in the hospital. Too late.

She reached for her glass with a shaky hand. For so long, everyone had insisted it wasn't her fault, that Louanne loved her. Perhaps she had a right to be angry at Dana, or wanting time to figure out things for herself, but terrible things could happen if you wasted time.

She didn't know what to do or believe anymore. Holly realized she'd left the beautiful necklace, created by an artist who would most likely lose her shop soon, up at Dana's house. For some reason, that made her cry harder.

Chapter Twenty-One

DANA

On the 26th, Dana started the coffee and then asked Annie to drop her off at Holly's. It was early, and impolite to bother people during the holidays, but she didn't care anymore. There was a distinct chance she could make the people of Chestnut Hill trust her, and not the way Marks' clients wanted her to. If she was honest, it was only one person's trust that counted, but the path to it was the same.

Holly looked tired and hung over, wearing a robe over PJs. She made no attempt at hiding her irritation when she learned the reason for Dana's visit.

"Really, you had to do this today?"

"I'm so sorry, but I need my car keys. I'll explain later." *If you let me*, she added silently.

Holly didn't comment, but she went to get Dana her keys.

"There you go."

"Thank you so much. I swear there's a good reason for this."

"All right. Have a good day." With a shrug, Holly closed the door.

Annie was waiting for Dana outside, leaning against her car. She didn't say anything, though her expression revealed her curiosity. Dana didn't have the time or inclination to indulge her.

"You can go back to the house."

"I don't know, I think I might go get some pastries from the bakery for breakfast."

"Sure, you do that. I'll see you later."

Dana finally got into her own car, eager to continue her mission.

She didn't give the person who was next on her list a chance to say anything first.

"You don't know me, but I need to talk to you. I'm aware that it's early, and you probably have other things to do than listen to me, but Holly won't, and I think you're the only one who can help me at this point."

Maddy Crawford's gaze was cool, not too friendly.

"I know who you are, Ms. Clover. If you thought I'd help you make those buys, I'm sorry, I can't help you."

"They shouldn't sell. That's what I'm trying to tell you. And I have something that will put them in a better position to refuse the offer."

"So you're admitting it's your firm's intent to rip off the residents of this town?"

Dana paused for a moment. It sounded bad—it described the situation exactly.

"I sent them my resignation...well, I had already resigned before I came here, but I told them I wouldn't be working for them on the deal. I want to represent the shop owners."

"Why would you do that?"

"Because I want Holly to know I'm capable of doing the right thing. Because I want to do the right thing." She'd have to deal with worse than Mrs. Crawford's suspicions eventually—she hadn't heard back from Marks regarding her decision yet.

Dana didn't regret it though. In the past twenty-four hours, the past week, her purpose had become much clearer. She would never be happy with Sheldon & Marks, the kind of clients they represented, the outcomes they favored. The people of Chestnut Hill had welcomed her, and now they needed her.

"I'm not even sure any of them could afford a fancy lawyer."

"They don't have to. I was looking for something new anyway, and...I guess I could always sell the house."

Crawford seemed to give that some thought, then she said, "Come on in. You're right—we should talk."

·♥·♥·♥·♥·♥·

Dana knew that coming here, to the house of Louanne's aunt, would either be a disaster, or the solution she'd been looking for. She was relieved to find that she was much closer to the latter. Maddy's house was filled with family, adults, children, some of them still enjoying breakfast.

Maddy had asked her into the kitchen where she poured two cups of coffee, setting one in front of Dana. There was still food on the table, the sight and smell distracting. Her host took notice.

"I hope you don't mind," she said, as she got two plates out of the cabinet. "I haven't had breakfast yet, and something tells me you haven't either. So please, help yourself to anything you like."

"Thank you." Dana chose a muffin, and after the first sip of coffee, she started laying out her strategy on how to defeat her former employer.

"I'm impressed," Maddy said. "You put this together quickly."

"They weren't about to let me go because I wasn't good. They wanted me to pay for someone else's mistake."

"I see. Do you mind if I ask you a personal question?"

Her love life was already the talk of the town, so how could she say no to the mayor?

"Go ahead. Please."

"I appreciate what you're trying to do. This might even work, but it makes me wonder, why did you want to get back with them in the first place?"

"If only I knew. I'd say it was a mistake, but then again, we'd have never found out about their real intention until it was too late." Dana sighed. "For a short time, I honestly thought this would be good for the people in town. And I imagined working on this project would show everyone that I was serious about staying, making a home here."

"Everyone?" Maddy raised an eyebrow.

"Well. Mostly...Holly. But everyone was great when I needed help, and I enjoy being here. It's not that I don't love the city, but I think I can do without it. I don't think Holly can do without Chestnut Hill."

"For sure, we wouldn't want to lose her. Nevertheless, that sounds like a big change. Would you be ready for that?"

The question made Dana feel foolish and naïve. Of course she'd be ready for that. She had dreamed about the life they could have together, and perhaps that included the occasional weekend in NYC...but her daydream had come to an end. Holly had rejected her.

"I'll see this through," she said. "Truth be told, I'm not exactly sure what's going to happen after that. I hope it means I'm still welcome here."

Again, Maddy understood what she'd said between the lines. But Holly might be the one who wasn't ready, and then what?

"Okay," Maddy said. "This is what we do. As you said, time is of the essence, so we'll disturb a few of the owners right now and have them come here. I have an endless supply of food and coffee, so that shouldn't be a problem. Talk to them, tell them about their options, and we'll go from there."

She didn't wait for an answer, just picked up her phone, scrolled through her address book, and called a number.

"Yes, this is Maddy Crawford. No, this is not a joke. It's about the firm wanting to build the resort—I need you to come to my house. We might have a solution. Yes, right now, why do you think I'm calling you?"

The next few calls went in a similar manner. Less than half an hour later, they were all set.

"I really hope you can do this," Maddy said wistfully. "You've only been here for a couple of weeks, but I can assure you, these people work hard, and they are trying to make their dreams come true. Those offers won't do much in the long run, and they will change the face of the town forever."

"Well, not all is said and done yet. Let's get to work. There's someone I need to disturb as well."

Chapter Twenty-Two

HOLLY

S he couldn't stand being alone in her house. Holly decided to go over to Marcie's, which was open today, even though most residents were still at home. A group of tourists, a family with two children, was sitting in one of the booths, two women in another. Holly found herself a place in the corner.

Lizzie wasn't working today, but a new girl. When Holly was halfway through her meal, Marcie came over to her table.

"Holly! I didn't expect you here today."

"Could you be any less subtle?" Holly wondered out loud. She didn't mind, and Marcie knew it. They both looked outside where a number of cars passed by, an unusual amount of traffic for this time of day. She recognized some. "What's going on there?"

"I'm not sure. Eliza was here a few minutes ago. Maddy asked her and others to go to her house. I thought you might know more."

Eliza was the artist who had sold Dana the necklace. Holly shook her head with a wry smile. "You know that I'm always the last to figure it out."

"Don't sell yourself short, honey. A lot has happened in the past few days."

"No kidding." Holly assumed that Maddy would be hunkering down with the shop owners, trying to come up with the best solution for everyone. Had she brushed Dana off too quickly? What if she could help?

What if Holly had to get over herself and put the fate of Chestnut Hill over her own sensibilities?

"But you're right, I should know more. This will potentially affect all of us. What if they're not satisfied with one block? The building I live in is old, but not that old. There are no protections."

"The same goes for most of us on this street. I hope we'll find out soon."

"What about now?" Holly got to her feet and tossed a bill onto the table. "I don't think there's a lot of time. I'll come back later and tell you what I found out."

"Sure...Thank you."

Holly was already out the door and on the way to her car. She had an idea.

·♥·♥·♥·♥·♥·

Maddy regarded her with an amused expression that seemed inappropriate for the gravity of the situation. At least, she didn't mind Holly crashing her meeting.

"Look, I know everything is really complicated right now, but I've been thinking. Dana said that she wanted to help—I wasn't sure how, or if it isn't too late already, but you seem to think that we can still do something, and that tells me we can. What if we hired her instead? If everyone came together, we could certainly afford it."

"Holly. Take a breath and come on in. The more the merrier."

"I'm serious. This could work," Holly insisted as she took off her coat.

"I've been thinking the same thing,"

She spun around to see Dana standing in the doorway. The mixed emotions were almost too much—Holly felt embarrassed and guilty about the way she'd left things, and her private meltdown, together with an odd sense of relief. Dana was okay—and why wouldn't she be? They'd have another chance to talk, work things out, after tackling the more acute challenge.

"So, am I right? Can we afford you?"

"Oh, you most certainly can. This is pro bono."

Holly felt her jaw drop. "Why? I mean, that's great, but I don't understand."

Maddy patted her shoulder. "I'll leave you to it. Come back in when you're ready."

Holly waited until they were alone, then she said, "Thank you. I mean it. Even if I don't understand."

"It's not so complicated. Chestnut Hill is important to me too. I know a bit about how this part of the real estate market works, and long-term—you just wouldn't benefit. They have their franchise, they bring in their own people, and a hotel complex like that has its own shops and restaurants. I wanted to be able to feel good about doing my job again. I believe I know what I have to do."

"That is great. It's amazing, in fact."

"We haven't won yet. But I know how Sheldon & Marks work, and if it becomes too much trouble, they'll drop the client before they walk away. Should we go inside?"

"Yes. Sure." She couldn't help the faint sense of disappointment. Wasn't there something else they should clear up while they had the chance? Priorities, Holly reminded herself. Once this problem was solved, perhaps another could be, too.

Chapter Twenty-Three

DANA

She wanted to pull Holly close and kiss her, make her forget about all the doubts. Dana knew she had to be careful and focus on what might become the most important case of her career. The business owners who had one by one filed into Maddy Crawford's den, had regarded her with suspicion at first—especially Eliza who had sold her the necklace. Her little shop was right at the center of the plans for the new hotel structure, as were several others.

Dana didn't want to disappoint any of them—she wouldn't be able to bear disappointing herself one more time. Every action she had taken since that fateful day seemed to have pointed her in the right direction, even the short time that she'd thought she could go back to Sheldon & Marks. Now, she had to put up. Her dream of making a home and a living here in Chestnut Hill could come true, but now the townspeople, who had welcomed her as a guest, had expectations.

She tried to avoid looking at Holly while she finished her presentation. It was yet to be determined if she could be in Dana's new life—but if she wasn't, what was the point?

When she stopped talking, everyone started at once. They had lots of questions. Dana almost didn't hear her cell phone, and when she realized who was calling, she held up a hand.

"I'm sorry, I will try to answer all your questions best I can, but I have to take this."

She stepped aside to accept the call, and then held the phone a few inches away from her ear as Marks started his angry tirade.

"Are you out of your damn mind, Clover? Do you know how much business this client will bring to us? Damn it, we should have fired you the first time. You have always been soft, and this just proves it."

It had become silent in the room.

"You might call it soft, but I'm looking out for my clients."

"Clients," he sneered. "Those morons wouldn't know what's good for them if you hit them over the head with it. I can't believe it only took you a few days to fall for those romantic delusions. That stupid little town is done! Do you hear me? Done!"

"I heard you loud and clear," Dana said. "And so did every single owner of the businesses you want to tear down after buying them for a ridiculously low price."

"Bitch! You set me up!" He had only now realized that she'd put him on speaker the moment he started yelling at her. Dana wasn't the only one who flinched at the expletive, but she had more to say to him.

"No, Mr. Marks. You did all of that to yourself. Well…you'll hear from me. I don't think a single one of them is still thinking about selling."

"You'll see, they have no choice. Those ridiculous regulations will be revoked."

"Right, about that. I have someone here who would like a word."

"Mr. Marks, I think you misunderstood something. These buildings are part of the local heritage, and they're protected for a reason," the congressman said. "I'm sure you understand."

Dana had no illusions as to why he'd had a change of heart, but it didn't matter at the moment.

When she ended the call, she saw nothing but determination in the faces of the residents gathered. What was even better, there was no more suspicion—but it was Holly's smile, when she finally dared to look at her, that gave her the most hope.

·▼·♥·♥·♥·▼·

After the meeting, everyone went to Marcie's, though to her chagrin, Dana didn't end up at the same table as Holly. She resigned to her fate and made some small talk with Eliza and another business owner, startled when Annie, Kristen and Tricia entered the café. Dana realized that Holly had noticed as well.

Annie and Kristen found a table of their own, while Tricia headed straight for Dana's table. Dana had mixed feelings—especially considering the audience.

"Hi. Dana, can I talk to you for a moment?"

"Sure."

They went over to the entrance and stood near a rack with brochures about Chestnut Hill.

"I wanted to apologize again," Tricia said.

"You helped save the town. I think you're forgiven by now."

"Still, I need to say it. I didn't know what I was thinking, just because it's Christmas... I'm glad it worked out and we could get the congressman on board." She smiled wryly. "Even though I doubt he's doing it out of the goodness of his heart."

"Today of all days I'm not going to question a miracle."

"I think that's a great way to look at it. Anyway…I'm going back. The whole idea was…let's say, I could have done better."

"I wish you all the best." Dana meant it. With a bit of distance, she could understand Tricia's reasoning, even though she'd gone about making her point all wrong.

"Thank you. And I promise you that if I come back to town every once in a while, it has nothing to do with you. I mean, we're adults—we can still say hi, right? Good luck, Dana. I hope everything works out well for you."

Dana was still trying out the more cryptic part of Tricia's words when her gaze fell on the bracelet she was wearing. The colors were different, but she recognized the style. Outside the door, Tricia waved, and it wasn't for Dana.

Perhaps Christmas miracles happened for everyone in Chestnut Hill.

·♥·♥·♥·♥·♥·

Dana excused herself and went over to Annie and Kristen.

"Hey," Annie said. "You still want to be seen with us in public, after we messed up things?"

"It could have been worse," Dana acknowledged. "No, really, it's okay. Tricia did help with the case. Did you know she was going home?"

"Yes. She got a rental car and said she didn't mind if we stayed as long as originally planned. That is, if you don't mind."

"Of course not. Even though I'll have work to do now."

"You don't need to entertain us," Kristen said. "It's a beautiful little town—and the food is amazing too."

"I'm glad to hear that." Marcie beamed as she brought their dessert. "So it's true? You're going to stay in Chestnut Hill?"

"I have to. My clients are here."

"That's all?"

"Um...Marcie. What did I tell you about interrogating guests?"

Everyone laughed before Marcie went to another guest who was ready to pay. Holly stood, seeming unsure about what to do next.

"That's not all," Dana told her and pointed to the empty seat next to her. "Please, join us, so we can finally do this the right way. Holly, these are my friends Annie and Kristen. Annie, Kristen...this is Holly who saved my life on the first day I came here. I think that's when I fell in love with her."

Holly blushed, but she sat. "I didn't know that was how you were going to introduce me."

"Do you mind?" Dana hoped she hadn't gone too far.

"Not at all."

Holly's kiss convinced her that she'd set the exact right tone.

·♥·♥·♥·♥·♥·

"So what are you going to do with the house?" Annie asked, later that night when they sat in Dana's living room with a nightcap, flames dancing in the fireplace.

Even though she knew that the following weeks would come with lots of work and decisions, Dana felt relaxed as never before, with Holly next to her, and her friends finally understanding that she wasn't going back.

"I'm not sure yet. If I want to continue to practice law, I should look for something in town."

"And you happen to know someone who has lots of space," Holly reminded her.

"True. I think I could rent it out—but now that the hotel is not going to get build, there could be interest in a little B&B..."

"I knew you wanted changes." Kristen sounded baffled. "I didn't know you wanted them to be this drastic."

"Like I said, I haven't decided yet, but I guess it makes sense to rent it out, and as soon as possible. I got my last paycheck from Sheldon & Marks."

"What if folks got together, and they pay you what they can?" Holly asked. "Meanwhile, we could get this place ready."

The "we" in her sentence warmed her more than the fire.

"It will be fine. It won't take long, just a little cleaning up...as long as I have somewhere to go."

"I promised you," Holly whispered.

Perhaps, Dana thought, she was never that bad at reading signs. The moment she had started to trust her intuition, the pieces had started to come together. She knew exactly where she needed to be, and with whom.

Chapter Twenty-Four

HOLLY

By New Year's Eve, Annie and Kristen had left. Dana and Holly had made a brief appearance at Marcie's party, where Dana took a moment to share the good news: An angry Marks had informed her that their client was going to back out of the deal and build their complex elsewhere.

Dana had taken the call on speaker, and Holly had overheard his final words—"And should you ever come back, I'll make sure you won't work anywhere in this city, ever again."

Dana didn't mind. She had a few options for an office she could look at, and several business owners that had approached her for representation. At some point, they had shared a look across the room, and without words, agreed that they wanted some time to themselves before the start of the New Year, and their new life together.

"Do you have any regrets?" Holly asked as they stood by the window, glasses ready.

"None whatsoever," Dana said, and they clinked their glasses together as the clock struck midnight. Her kiss left Holly with no doubt.

"You?"

"No. I know that this is right."

As if on cue, down in Chestnut Hill, the fireworks began.

·♥·♥·♥·♥·♥·

Busy times were ahead for both of them, but Dana still had some things to wrap up. Holly found a temporary replacement, a doctor she'd worked with together at St. Christopher's before, and she accompanied Dana to New York to help her tie up lose ends.

She couldn't help it, her jaw dropped a little when she first stepped into Dana's apartment.

Dana, leaning against the doorframe, watched her with a soft smile.

"Would you prefer we live here?" She knew the answer already. They had talked at length about this.

"I just want to make *us* work. Everything else, we figure out, right?"

"Yeah. Marks talks a big game, but they don't have that much power. I made up my mind. That, and I already accepted Kristen and Annie's purchase offer. We better start packing."

Kristen and Annie would move into the apartment. They had agreed to take some of the furniture, and what wouldn't travel back with Dana and Holly in boxes, they'd give to charity.

This was the longest time Holly had ever taken off in her entire career, and she cherished every moment, every new experience—while she knew there was only one place that would ever feel like home to her, and now, even more.

·♥·♥·♥·♥·♥·

They went to a restaurant located on the top floor of a skyscraper with Kristen and Annie that night. At times, Holly had a hard time thinking that Dana was ready to give up all of this to come live with her in Chestnut Hill, but Dana was confident, and sure about her decision.

"I know what you're thinking," she said. "I'm ready for a pace that's a little less crazy. And it's not like we can't ever come back."

"Well, I hope you'll be back every once in a while, and visit your goddaughter..." Annie said.

Holly and Dana sat in stunned silence, before they remembered their manners, and hugs and congratulations ensued.

Chapter Twenty-Five

DANA

After all practical manners were taken care of, Dana took the time to show Holly around, all the parts of the city that had never been associated with heartbreak or disappointments.

They bundled up to take walks in Central Park and braved the lines at the Met. Dana realized that she was filled with the same excitement she'd felt when she first moved here, and then came to work with Sheldon & Marks. Only now, she was excited about going home...

Epilogue

CHRISTMAS, ONE YEAR LATER

"A re you nervous?" Dana asked when she fastened the necklace for Holly, searching her gaze in the mirror.

Perhaps, nervous wasn't the right word, Holly reflected. Butterflies in her stomach. Excitement. Yes, perhaps she was nervous as well, even though she knew that everyone would greet them with kindness.

The past year had come with many challenges, keeping up her practice, Dana starting hers, and the two of them renting out the house on the hill to many happy tourists. They had made time to talk, to breathe...to love. Come next summer, they had even bigger plans, but she couldn't get too far ahead of herself...

In a matter of minutes, they'd leave for Maddy Crawford's annual Christmas party. The ring on Holly's finger wouldn't be a surprise to any of the guests—everyone knew she and Dana were inseparable and had been since they had returned from New York.

"I'm good if you are."

Dana gave her the once over, and whispered, "Perfect. Merry Christmas."

This time, it was true.

About the Author

Barbara Winkes writes sapphic crime drama and Christmas romance. She loves writing characters who get the job done, whether it's stopping a predator or saving cherished traditions—while still making time for love. She lives with her wife in Quebec City.

barbarawinkes.com